THE ROAD HOME

WHEN COMING HOME IS MORE PAINFUL THAN LEAVING.

SHANA GRAY

1

———

The Road Home
Shana Gray

She was coming home. Back where she grew up and spent so many years with Gram in the bakery. The road home had been a long one. Kara dreaded seeing what kind of shape the shop and apartment were in now, not having been used or lived in for so long. Guilt soured in her stomach. No matter how hard she'd tried to justify staying away, it hadn't been the right decision. She should have come back sooner, and whispered a silent apology to Gram.

On the heels of her memory of Gram came one of a dark-haired, dreamy-faced boy from long ago, which made her sit upright in her rental car. Even though it had been years since she'd seen him, he still haunted her thoughts. She sighed. Of course he *would* cross her mind now, since reminders were everywhere.

Her breasts tingled. Even after all these years, her body

responded to his memory. His first tentative touch when they were teenagers had overwhelmed her. She'd lost herself in his chocolate-brown eyes and under his touch when they gave their virginity to each other. A summer love from so long ago still held the same power over her now as it did then.

"Max." His name rolled off her tongue and she gripped the steering wheel tighter when her belly did a little flip-flop. She didn't know if he'd stayed on his family's orchard, and whether they still ran the fruit market. Maybe he had realized his dream to turn it into a profitable winemaking operation. Niagara-on-the-Lake had a thriving wine business.

It had been difficult to make herself Google Maxwell Grimes Stone II for two reasons. One was her focus on her own culinary career, and the other had been something she still refused to think about and a big reason she'd stayed away for so long. But resist she did. Had Max ever found out what had really made her decide to leave?

She knew she'd broken his heart when she ran off to Europe fifteen years ago. Her own heart had been in tatters when ran away to learn her craft, leaving a very confused and angry Max behind. Gram had told her he pined for her and encouraged her to contact him, but she couldn't bring herself to do that. He'd never tried to get in touch with her, either. When the news of his marriage to Patricia Howe reached her, she'd cried for days, and once the wailing was done Kara firmly put Maxwell Stone on the shelf. She had to in order to keep her focus.

She glanced out the window of the car at the passing scenery. She'd managed to keep thoughts of him at bay-- well, most of the time. Sleep was where he visited her. In her dreams, where he was a lovely fantasy she welcomed with open arms. But waking up the next morning always left her feeling empty and lost.

Time had slipped by quickly and when Gram died suddenly last year, everything seemed to come crashing down around her. Kara drew in a shaky breath remembering the whirlwind of Gram's funeral, sorting out her affairs and being afraid she'd stumble across Max. Once she'd returned to France, she'd finally admitted that she needed to come back home.

Now here she was, driving the familiar roads of Niagara-on-the-Lake on the way to her childhood home.

The flight from Paris to Toronto had been uneventful, yet she'd been agitated most of the time she was in the air but was unable to pinpoint her unease. Kara groaned and swallowed a wave of nausea.

Why? Because I might see him or because I might not?

Kara forced her thoughts away from Max as she exited the Queen Elizabeth Way. Time enough to think about him later. She had a goal and her timeline was tight. No distractions allowed. Coming home to reopen the bakery excited her and was foremost in her mind. After closing the shop last year, she expected to be in for a good cleanup. Even though she'd had the place checked on regularly, Kara was sure it needed some tender loving care and she was here to provide just that.

As she drove deeper into the region, she couldn't believe how many vineyards had sprung up. She drove past the familiar Hillebrand and Jackson Triggs wineries, as well as a sprawling new one that didn't even resemble a winery—it rose out of the earth like a monolith, all chrome and glass except for the telltale rows of vines fanning out on each side. She could barely take it all in. Sure, she was on the same old Niagara Stone Road but oh, man, had it changed.

Inniskillin, which had basically started the Niagara wine industry back in 1975, was on the western edge of the region, close to the Niagara River. *Where we'd found a private little hidey-hole to explore each other... Stop it, Kara! Quit with the thoughts already.*

This wasn't a good sign. Max crossing her mind was never good—it roused images of him and set her long-neglected libido aflutter. She needed a man. Wanted one. But purely for sex. The complications of a relationship she could do without. But sex? Yup, scratch that itch and be on her way. Maybe a nice Canadian boy would walk into her shop and tempt her. She laughed out loud and promised herself she wouldn't let her hopes get too high.

With her destination just around the corner, Kara realized she was holding her breath and let it out slowly through pursed lips. She turned onto Queen Street and drove right into Old Town. Her chest swelled and emotion for her hometown filled her.

She was here.

Home.

The gracious old trees shaded the road, and flowers of every kind exploded with brilliant color along the sidewalks, in flower beds, in planters, hanging pots —and it was glorious!

Typical for a weekday in July, the street was jam-packed with people, and typically there was no parking. Tourists flowed along the sidewalks, horses pulling carriages clip-clopped down the street, sightseers gazed into shop windows or sat at one of the many outdoor cafés, sipping wine from area vineyards and noshing on locally grown foods. Niagara-on-the-Lake was a one-of-a-kind place to indulge one's culinary senses and the place that had originally inspired Kara to become a chef.

She loved it here. Why, oh, why had she waited so long before coming back? But she knew the answer to that. It was the combination of avoiding Max and getting her own career on track. She realized now that it had been wrong and she should have settled here long ago like she'd promised Gram; instead she'd let herself get wrapped up in the glitzy worlds of Paris and London. It was hard to face being back now with Gram gone, hard to accept that working side by side with her again would never be.

She shook her head, refusing to let the sad thoughts take hold, and drove slowly, watching for the storefront. There! On the left, set back from the road. She'd almost missed the red-and-cream brick of the old building, and the black framed windows. The patio was wild with overgrown vines and jolts of color from the perennials Gram had planted so many years ago. It really needed some TLC. Being set back from the road was a treasure, and it created a nice little spot for café tables, with a hedge acting as a fence between the patio and sidewalk. It also sorely needed tending. Everything looked tired and unloved now, unlike the rest of the shops, and a pang of embarrassment touched her. The old sign above the rolled-up awning had peeled just enough to reveal the original lettering underneath. *Fingertips.* The name Gram gave the bakery all those years ago when she opened it. She said love was in her fingertips when she baked.

Kara's heart constricted. She swallowed the lump in her throat. "Oh, Gram. I'm so sorry." She craned her neck to watch the store disappear in her rearview mirror and swung her gaze back to the road just in time and stomped on the brakes to avoid running up the back end of a stopped car. *Sheesh, pay attention.*

"Move it, buddy." Kara punched the horn. Some things

never changed and traffic was one. Cars double-parked and bunged up traffic while the passengers climbed out excruciatingly slowly. Now that she'd arrived, Kara was in no mood for tolerance. She tapped her thumbs on the steering wheel.

Summer in Old Town was nuts, and this was just the beginning. She'd planned wisely, arriving after the Canada Day weekend, which coincided with July 4th. People from around the world flocked to Niagara Falls and Niagara-on-the-Lake, and the little town was almost bursting at the seams. There was chaos all around. But this was also a short season, so she took it all in stride.

Kara sucked in a deep breath and rested her elbow on the door, waiting for the car ahead to move. Intolerant drivers from behind began a chorus of honking and finally the car pulled away. Kara followed a little too closely, impatient to get to the shop. The upcoming stoplight turn green. She flicked on her indicator signal and took a risky turn ahead of a van coming from the opposite direction, which flashed its high beams at her.

She waved an apology and watched for the entrance to the private parking area in a laneway behind the buildings. She licked her lips, which were dry from nervous excitement. She crept forward, eagerly watching for the back of the bakery, and pulled in. Then she sat in the car for a minute, gazing at the familiar old building where she'd grown up.

It hadn't changed all that much from the outside. The bushes and neighboring trees were bigger, a little wilder, and sheltered the back door of the shop. It was difficult to see the second-floor deck from the overhanging branches. That could be a good thing. Privacy from prying eyes.

Kara finally climbed out of the car and stood at the back door, jangling the keys in her hand. What was she waiting for? Why the hesitation? She'd come all this way to start a new life and now here she was. All it would take was putting the key in the lock, pushing open the door and taking one step across the threshold. Her new life would begin behind that closed door.

She glanced at the antique black iron urn, which weighed a ton, that still stood sentry by the door. A lonely-looking thing now, all by itself, flowerless, on the little stone patio. Kara pulled out the old, dried-up leaves. Soon it would be full of blooms. She nodded her head. Yep. Soon her new home would be rejuvenated. Refreshed. And ready for the world.

The keys weighed heavy in her hand and she picked through them to find the right one. It slid into the lock and turned without protest. Pausing to draw in a breath, she leaned on the door and it opened easily. Almost as if it were welcoming her.

Hushed silence greeted her. Kara's eyes adjusted to the dim light before she stepped past the vestibule into the kitchen and looked around.

"Oh, my." Raising a hand to her throat, she took it all in. Sunlight filtered through the closed shutters, casting an eerie light, and dust motes danced on the rays. Ghostly white sheets covered everything. Nothing had been touched since her last visit when she'd closed the place down. Standing in the center of the room, she slowly turned around. Gram's bakery. Now hers.

She reached out and her fingertips played with the corner of a drop sheet. Kara took a deep breath and pulled away the fabric inch by inch until the island workstation was revealed, its surface a combination of marble and stainless steel. She yanked off the second sheet covering the far end. An ethereal image of her as a child, standing on an old chair pushing a rolling pin over pastry with Gram at her side, played before her on the dusty air. Then it floated away.

Unable to hold back the tears any longer, she cried, clutching the white sheet to her as great sobs almost tore her apart.

She cried for her parents that died when she was a baby, for Gram's love and patience in raising her, for lost love and loneliness. Despair washed over her and she let it feed her tears. She was alone in the world. This was the first time she'd cried about everything she'd lost. How she longed for someone to hold her, to cry on a comforting shoulder.

A few minutes later, she wiped her hand across her cheeks and blew her nose into a corner of the sheet. *Get it together, Kara.* She wasn't a crier, but this crying jag was long overdue and maybe she did feel a little better.

Kara tossed the balled-up sheet aside and turned around to flip the lights on. A shadowy figure stood in the doorway and her heart tripped over itself. "Who are you?"

2

"I heard you were back in town." A deep familiar voice tickled her senses, sending a delicious shiver along the backs of her arms.

Max! Kara stood frozen, totally confused by his presence. Had she conjured him up, thinking about him on the drive here? Her breath stopped and no words formed. A crazy thought of how horrible she must look and she reached up to smooth a wayward strand of hair.

He stepped into the beams of dancing light. His smile, wide and welcoming, and his eyes—the color of warm chocolate syrup—weakened Kara's knees.

"Oh, Max." Kara ran to him and threw her arms around his neck. He lifted her easily off the ground. A low chuckle rumbled from his broad chest and she wound her arms around his neck hugging him as if to never let him go. Here was the strong shoulder she needed.

Gone was the gangly teenage boy and in his place was a strong, mature and very solidly muscled man. He swung her around until she giggled. Her despair from only a moment ago vanished and a glimmer of happiness sprouted.

"Hey, gorgeous. It's good to see you." He set her down and held her away from him, keeping his hands on her shoulders. She shivered when his gaze swept from her toes to her face. Geez, she still responded to him like a virgin teen and her nipples had stiffened under her sleeveless blouse. She pushed a curl off her face, not because it was bothersome, but because suddenly she was shy and nervous.

He smiled. There was no need to be nervous around Max and she liked the genuine delight she saw in his eyes before his face clouded. "I was so sorry to hear about Gram."

"Thanks." The underlying sadness that had haunted her for the past year and a half surfaced with those few words, but she didn't want to repeat her feelings of moments before. It was so good to see him. She was tongue-tied all of a sudden. He must have sensed it and let her go.

"How did you know I was here?"

"It's a small town, Kara. Everyone knows everything."

She nodded. True enough. She'd kept in contact with the lawyers and made arrangements through them to have the building checked on regularly. People talked.

"This old place sure brings back memories." He strode through the kitchen out to the shop proper and Kara followed him. Seeing him here now, so unexpectedly, made her realize how much she'd missed him. He had matured nicely and filled the room with his presence, as if he belonged here. His trim hips and broad shoulders were so much more muscular now, and his butt, the same wonderful ass, fantastic in any pair of jeans, caught her attention. She allowed herself a moment to appreciate the tempting outline behind the denim. *Whoa, settle down.*

Lord, the sight of him still cast a spell over her. He moved around the store with the same easy gait, only now he was even more spellbinding. If she wasn't careful, she'd start fantasizing them together...

"I think I can still smell the butter and pastries." He placed his hand on the still shrouded bakery display case.

Kara blinked away her growing daydream. She sniffed, holding her breath and yes, it was there--the scent of baking. Wow, she was stunned. Was it real or were they imagining it?

"Um, m-maybe." To still smell the baking of bygone days seemed surreal. All the years of her youth flashed by, and her chest tightened. *Gram. She really is gone.* and being here in the closed up bakery drove it home like a spike through her heart. Lost years that could never be replaced.

Hushed silence surrounded them. Kara glanced at Max and saw that he was looking off, as if lost in his own memories. Everyone had called Gram *Gram.* She'd been the unofficial granny to most of her friends. When they were kids and Gram always had a plate of something special waiting for them after school. Memories of the gang sitting on the patio flooded her. She'd lost track of everyone when she'd moved to France and hadn't had time to reconnect since coming home.

Then he murmured, snapping her out of her thoughts. "The walls must have soaked up all those years of Gram's baking." He reached for one of the shutters and unhooked it.

"Please, Max, no. Not yet."

He looked over his shoulder. "Why, what's up?" His easy-going nature was still there under the layers of manhood, but he had a different air about him. Confident. No-nonsense and strong. A rousing combination to be sure.

"I'm not ready for the world to come in yet," she whispered and glanced at the shuttered windows.

He looked puzzled. "You're here now, and it's not a secret." His voice was gentle, which edged her close to tears again.

Kara sighed. Standing in the center of the shop, she slowly turned as she had in the kitchen. The long glass counter, which ran the length of the store in front of the old stone wall, was still asleep under the drop sheets. The antique maple display shelves on the opposite wall were also draped with a sheet. A cluster of humps looked like a colony of mushrooms hunched by the front windows, but they were just the cast iron outdoor furniture she'd dragged in off the patio the last time she was here. Gram's cozy wing chairs were tucked into the corner.

"I know, but it's important to bring everything back as if she's still here." Kara stepped to the counter and pulled the sheets off.

The beautiful beveled glass and ornate carved wood counter was revealed. She sucked in a soft gasp, remembering the mouthwatering show of pastries, cakes, tarts and pies, buns and breads that used to sit in this old display case, waiting for people to take them home. She could almost taste them.

"I'll bring it all back, Max, and it will be even better." Now, a little more determined, Kara faced him.

He nodded, watching her from across the room. Their eyes met. Her heart beat double time when he grinned, revealing that devilish dimple in his cheek. "I know you will."

She let out a sigh and curled her arms around her body.

"I want to keep the antique feel but modernized. Turn it into a gathering place. Good food, coffee, teas and if I can get a liquor license, wine too. Bakery by day and wine bar by night. With internet access. Hopefully that will bring the crowds back."

"I don't think you have to worry about that. All those extras would only be for the tourists." His eyes held a deeper meaning that set her belly quivering. "We've been waiting for you to come home." His voice was low and intimate.

She paused in the middle of folding the sheet. Her eyelids fluttered for a moment as a wave of delight trembled through her. He'd said "we" but she heard "I. Unsure how to respond, she smiled at his comment.

She needed to know more, though, and bit her tongue to hold back the inquiring words she was dying to ask. Why was he here? Did he know what had happened before she left? Had he been waiting for her to come back? Had he missed her? A fleeting thought of his marriage pulled her up short. No, she wasn't ready to know more about his nuptials.

She felt a shift inside her from how she'd felt just a few hours ago. All her determination had been focused on getting Fingertips back open and now, in a few short minutes, Max had become a delightful and potential diversion. But was he a diversion who'd distract her too much?

Kara walked toward him, keeping eye contact. She embraced the rousing desire, but wasn't ready to completely let her guard down. Placing the half-folded sheet on a shelf, she slipped between him and the shrouded furniture, which wasn't the easiest thing to do. She'd rather jump into his arms; instead she parted the old wooden slatted blinds a little so she could see out. She really wasn't paying attention to what was on the other side. All her nerves were on high alert because of Max. She sensed him behind her and a delicious shiver rippled along her spine to settle in hot tendrils around the base. Kara felt a need to fill the tension with mindless chatter and said the first thing that popped into her mind.

"Does Niagara College still have their horticulture program? Maybe some students would like to help bring the patio garden back to life."

"Mm, hmm, they do and they might."

He was right behind her. She felt him. All she had to do was lean back, and she wavered at the thought.

She forgot everything when Max's arm slid around her waist and his fingers splayed over her belly.

"Ooh…" Her eyes closed and she savored the sensation of his muscled chest against her back, the power in his embrace, and she rested her fingers on his forearm. It had been so long since she'd allowed these emotions to surface, and she let the thrill of his nearness envelope her.

He felt so good, and she sagged against him, as the blood rushing through her veins weakened her. Max's breath, so close to her ear, fluttered her hair. It was as if no time at all had passed They still fit together perfectly, as the way they had as teenagers.

He was much taller now and her head fit under his chin with a little more room than it had before. Was her curly hair tickling his nose, like it had all those years ago? A sudden sense of belonging struck her, and she leaned back into him, his solid muscles feeling so impenetrable, but she still melded perfectly to him. Kara liked the way his energy embraced her and she let it.

"Why, you thinking of getting a student to tidy it up?" he asked.

She nodded and murmured, "The thought just crossed my mind. It would give me more time to focus inside."

There was no denying that her attraction to him was still ripe. But then, why wouldn't it be? They'd had chemistry as teenagers and wouldn't it only grow through the years, especially with the distance between them. They'd never resolved the situation, and so the connection was still there...

Max had awakened her sexually, they'd fallen in love and explored each other. Knowing exactly how each needed to be touched. What pleased them. They'd shared their innermost thoughts. Grew together until they were ripped apart.

Kara pushed the anxiety-driven thoughts aside. She was still confused as to how she should handle herself, since the perfection of being together now was far more powerful. Her bar was set very high for any other man Kara allowed into her world. None of them could compare to Max.

She tightened her grip on his forearm and wanted to hug him tighter. Part of the reason she'd taken off fifteen years ago was because of her weakness. How could she stay, with Max so close, and not be able to be with him? With his mother watching everything they did like a hawk and with the threat of her making Kara's life miserable, it would have been impossible—eventually breaking them up if she'd stayed.

It felt so damn good to be back in his arms now, however casual it might be. She couldn't give in to the desires he so easily aroused, probably without realizing it.

She reminded herself again that he had a wife and she would never allow herself to be the *other woman*.

She had to remain focused on her goal. And keep simplicity in her life. The thought of his mother chilled her. Kara extricated herself from his strong arms, feeling an intense and immediate sense of loss. She walked between him and the tables looking for something to busy her hands with. Had he ever found out what really happened? What had prompted her to leave in the first place?

"Kara." His voice was thick.

"Uh, huh?" She fussed with the folded sheet, her back still to him. *Here it comes*, she thought.

"Kara, turn around." She heard the floorboards creak when he stepped closer to her.

Slowly she turned to face him. Seeing his oh, so familiar face, now so much more mature, a million thoughts raced through her mind, as her gaze searched him, she noticed the fine lines at the edges of his eyes and a wrinkle between his eyebrows. His skin was weathered, tanned, likely from his time in the sun tending his land. Which also had turned him into a lean and muscular figure. She drew in a soft breath. He was home. He was safety. He was peace.

He was her first love, and lover.

Her body remembered him well and she had to lock her knees so they wouldn't wobble. The familiar ache in her heart blended in perfect harmony with her arousal for him and no matter how hard she tried, she couldn't keep it at bay.

Putting an ocean between them had been the wisest thing she could have done. Maybe coming home was wrong, after all. She shook her head and stared at the item she'd picked up without really seeing it. Deep in her soul, she knew it wasn't wrong, for hers and Gram's sake. Coming home was right. For many reasons.

They had been perfect together *then*. Now was a whole other matter.

Why, oh, why was coming home more painful than leaving?

3

Kara wanted to be here, but she didn't want to remember the hurtful words that had been said to her, the words that had driven her away, but they came back like a punch in the gut. She'd built a new life abroad and survived. Her career became her passion and she poured everything into it, all the while carefully protecting herself from further heartache. Sure, there had been other men, but the wall she'd built around her heart was impenetrable and no one could compare to Max.

The best thing to do now was to step away. She was here to reopen Fingertips, using all the skills and business savvy she'd learned in France. Kara didn't need his mother's toxic presence poisoning her world. That woman was like a bad penny, always showing up at the wrong times ready to cause trouble. Kara fully expected the woman to make her life miserable in every way possible. There was only one thing she could do to protect herself.

Max stepped toward her and she stiffened, raising her hand. He halted in his tracks. "Kara, please, I think we should talk." The pained expression on his face told her he still didn't know what had happened all those years ago.

"Oh, Max, I just got home. Can't it wait?" Desperate now to maintain her space, she walked to the kitchen--and he followed.

His laugh sounded bitter. "For what? Come on, don't you think we have lots to discuss?"

She turned to him and met his gaze. "Maybe, but not right now."

His eyebrows shot up. She knew exactly what he wanted to talk about. But she wasn't ready. She'd just gotten home, for crying out loud, and already conflict was building. She wanted to find out about Patricia, his wife, but if she brought the subject up, it would launch into the whole drama of why'd she left to begin with. Now wasn't the time. She was exhausted and beginning to feel emotionally wrung out. Being here in the bakery without Gram broke her heart and Max standing before her--well, it was just too much to take in right now.

"It was really nice of you to stop by, but I-I think maybe you should leave." She couldn't look at him, positive that disappointment would show in his face.

"Is that what you really want?" His voice had an edge, and she couldn't help looking at him now.

No! I want you to stay and be with me. The words were so close to bursting forth.

"It's for the best, Max. So many years have gone by." Her lips were stiff and she struggled to force the words from between them. It was hard to send him away and she reminded herself she hadn't come back for Max, she'd come back to start a new life here.

His features hardened and it pained her. She didn't want to hurt him again, but she knew she was doing just that.

There was so much she had to do, and trying to fix, build, whatever...an old relationship was impossible.

He was married.

"One day I'd like you to tell me why you left."

And before she could say anything further, he walked past her and out the back door, taking with him the energy that seemed to swell in his presence. Suddenly the old bakery seemed empty and soulless without him.

This brief interlude with him after all these years made her realize what he still meant to her. She was torn now. And she asked herself again--should she have stayed overseas, or was coming home the right thing to do? If only she'd been strong enough to stand up to his mother and tell her to go to hell, things could have been so different for both of them. Kara drew in a big breath and stood tall. It was time to be honest with herself.

She still loved him.

M ax shut the truck door and rested his hands on the steering wheel. He sucked in a deep breath. That hadn't been easy, seeing Kara after all these years. But shit, it was good to see her and hold her again.

The few brief moments she'd been in his arms with her head tucked under his chin had sent him careening back in time. He'd felt like a school kid again, all giddy with new love and fiery hormones. She woke him up. He suddenly realized how desensitized he'd become over the years when the rush of raw desire for her ignited in his blood, his nostrils cleared and colors took on a new intensity. He felt good... No, great. A short burst of laughter erupted from him.

Even if she'd basically thrown him out and pretty much stated she wanted nothing to do with him, Kara breathed new life into his husk of a body. For the first time in a long time, a sense of hope took hold and a seed was planted.

He'd be back to win her over, even if only as friends. But first he'd let her do her thing and maybe, just maybe, she might miss him a little bit. And when that crack appeared, he'd slip right in.

4

"Wow." Kara drove up the neat paved driveway lined with row upon row of grapevines. She came to a Y just around a curve in the laneway and stopped, staring at a stunning house with a fantastic wraparound porch. Old maple and oak trees leaned over the porch roof, casting welcoming shadows in the heat of the day. To the left were similarly designed buildings, which must be the vineyard office and store. Kara turned left.

She gulped air, needing to slow down her heart. She hated that she was nervous. Once she'd found a parking space in front of the building, she sat in the car for a minute.

When she opened the door, the wonderful scent of flowers and warm earth filled her car, which sent her back through the years to when they were teens.

But that was so many years ago. She got out and ducked into the backseat, reaching for the large white bakery box full of treats that were his favorites. She hadn't forgotten, and that bugged the hell out of her. Bringing them over was an excuse to visit Max without calling first; it was also meant to be an apology for basically kicking him out the other day.

She climbed the winery shop's wide limestone steps, taking in the grandeur of the structure. It was beautiful. A wraparound porch, similar in style to the one at the house, led to an opening at the side; it was like an outdoor lounge, where a grouping of Muskoka chairs and low tables with fire pits were scattered about.

Kara took a deep breath and pushed open the tall, highly glossed wooden doors. She gasped. The spacious shop was beautiful and welcoming with slate floors and muted-tone walls. Gleaming counters, and the same glossy wood, accented with polished chrome and glass shelves ran along the walls lined with wine bottles beautifully lit with pot lights. Kara turned in a circle, taking it all in. The refrigerators with their glass doors blended perfectly with the décor and showcased wine.

"Oh, my." The view through the floor-to-ceiling windows was breathtaking. If she didn't know better, Kara would have thought she was looking at a mature vineyard in France or Italy.

But she wasn't. This was Max's winery, he'd really done well and brought the family business to new heights. She was more than impressed.

"Can I help you?"

Kara turned to the voice behind her. "Hello. Yes, please. I, um, is Max available?"

"No, I'm sorry. He's in a meeting at present. Is there something I can do for you?"

"Ah, well, can you please see he gets this box?" She held it out to the woman.

"Of course. Whom may I tell him this is from?"

Kara smiled. "He'll know. Thank you."

She wandered back out to the veranda and wanted to take a peek at the outdoor lounge she'd spied earlier. When she rounded the corner, a lovely breeze blew past her. There was nothing like the smell of the earth with the hot sun warming it. She inhaled the sweet air. What a great place to sit and take in the panorama with a glass of wine. It also had real potential as an outdoor café. Shielded from the elements, it offered a million-dollar view. She stood at the edge of the deck and saw the grand house partially visible through the trees. It looked spectacular from this angle as well.

"Kara." Oh, that voice, how it got under her skin, in a good way.

She smiled and turned to him. "Hi." Wind blew curls across her face and she peered at him through the strands.

They both spoke at the same time and laughed.

"You first," he said.

"I was told you were in a meeting." She pushed her hair from her forehead and held it while shielding her eyes from the sun.

"Yes, I was. I am. But I saw you through the window and excused myself. You're on my land now and no way was I going to let you leave without saying hello."

She glanced at the wall he indicated. She saw shadows behind the darkened panes of glass, people sitting around a conference table. He placed his hand on her elbow and led her off the deck behind a rose bush covered in fragrant pink blooms. A thrill tingled down her arm at his touch and she gently pulled from his grip.

"What a gorgeous place, Max. It's wonderful here." A pang of regret rose. If she'd stayed, they could have built this together.

He rocked back on his heels, a look of pleasure crossing his face. He looked out over his land. "I kind of agree."

She took the opportunity to really look at him. He was

her long-lost love, her teenage dream. He was the same, but oh, so different. Still her Max, but all grown up, and still a sexy beast. She cleared her throat, stemming her wayward thoughts but allowing herself one more appreciative glance and he caught it when his attention came back to her.

They paused and stared at each other. Kara held her breath, only to let it go when her heart skipped a beat. She wondered if his wife was close by and took a step back from him, needing to keep space between them. Why had she come here? Oh, yes, the box.

"I was rude the other day and I wanted to apologize." He smiled and her heart flipped over. She looked up at a heavy bloom and gently pulled it to her nose, sniffing the sweet scent. She glanced back at him. "Um...there's a box of goodies for you inside."

"Thanks. You didn't have to do that." He stepped closer. Kara didn't move, and the next thing she knew, she was wrapped in his arms. "I'm glad you stopped by. But I do have to get back to the meeting."

She let him hug her, released the flower and slid her arms around him, resting her cheek on his chest. She tried to make it a simple, friendly hug, but it was hard not to cling. He felt and smelled so damn good.

"No worries." Her words were muffled against the fine cotton of his dress shirt. She released her grip and moved to step away, but he hugged tight for a second longer before letting her go. "Take them into your meeting."

They mounted the steps to the open-air lounge and walked through to the parking lot. "Take what? Oh! The box of pastries. Sure." He held the car door open for her and she slid onto the seat. "Sorry I'm tied up right now."

He blocked the sun, and she looked up at him. "That's

okay. I'm busy, too. Just wanted to drop by quickly." Kara started the car. "We'll catch up eventually."

She pulled the door shut, sealing herself inside, safe from the temptation of him. She waved and drove off, letting out a breath. She glanced at him in the rearview mirror and wondered if they could just be friends. But if she were his wife, no way would she be up for her husband having a friendship with an old flame. That was like lighting a match to a stick. Kara sighed, the good feeling she'd momentarily experienced in his arms fading the further she drove away.

5

———

It hadn't taken the two students long to bring the patio gardens back to their former glory. They'd worked hard and finished it after a week. Since it was well into planting season, the college's greenhouses were full of mature plants that filled in the gardens. If Kara did say so herself, they looked so much better. The students planned to turn her exterior renovation into a semester project, which meant she wasn't required to pay them for anything but the plants and supplies. But she had every intention of compensating them for the work. They'd done a marvelous job, even tackling the jungle that was the second-level deck at the back of the building, off the apartment above the bakery she was now living in.

The other day Kara was startled to see people on the patio. She'd gone out to see what was going on. Tourists were taking photos. She'd quickly brought out some small pastries for them, as a thank you for their interest. As the plants filled in under the care of the students, the patio was becoming quite a splash of color. It made her smile to see the flow of picture-takers and she knew Gram would've been delighted by the rekindled interest in the bakery. She put up a small sign with the grand opening details.

She pulled all the café tables and chairs onto the patio for two reasons. One, so people could rest their aching feet, since seating was at a premium. And two, goodwill never hurt, and she hoped it would encourage them to return for her opening. Soon the shady rest stop was busy most of the day. The comings and goings of tourists seeking shade under the umbrellas and the maple tree growing from the center of the patio. Even dogs accompanying their owners became a fixture, and Kara made sure numerous water bowls were filled to the brim.

Only a little over a week until the doors to Fingertips reopened. The more she thought about it, the more her nerves played inside her stomach, and she did her best not to get too stressed. She couldn't eat or sleep and lived off coffee and water until her students forced her to sit down and eat. They were good kids, and she'd miss them when they returned to class.

Today had been exceptionally busy and the morning sped by. She needed a break and strolled down Queen Street to check out some of the other shops. When storekeepers saw her, they nodded or waved, gestures she returned. It really did feel good to be back.

It was a glorious day as she sauntered along the sidewalk, gazing in store windows. Outside a little shop, the song of wind chimes drew her over to the display. She couldn't reach the ones the ones hanging on the lower branches in the ancient tree, and turned to slowly spin the sidewalk display which held more chimes, until she found the ones she wanted. They were perfect for the patio. Untangling them from each other, caused a chorus of ringing as she chose a couple that were pretty and sparkly.

"I think this one's the best," a deep, sexy voice whispered next to her ear and a muscled arm reached across her shoulder. Kara froze and closed her eyes, enjoying the delightful shiver that trilled along her flesh. She knew exactly who the voice and arm belonged to, and turned to face Max. Damn if her heart didn't melt. She smiled, watching him extricate the large, gaudy chime from the others with no lack of noise.

"The rooster?" It was so good to see him and she did her best to contain her joy, although it was hard and a smile widened on her lips.

"Yeah, he's great." He finally got it unhooked from the branch. "My treat."

"Okay. A little whimsy never hurt anything." She was still smiling when he handed her the chime as they walked into the touristy store to pay.

Back outside they wandered down the street, shoulder to shoulder, the bag of chimes knocking against her leg. At times they had to shuffle tightly together or she'd have to step in front of him to squeeze through the crowd. His nearness triggered all sorts of emotions in her. His scent and the heat from his body played havoc with her senses. She was totally in tune with him and her sexual antenna was all abuzz. A sultry, satiny fluidness flowed through her veins--a sexiness she hadn't felt in oh, so long and she welcomed it, even when her breath quickened. It felt good to feel again. To feel like a woman. A woman beside her man. Her step faltered. He wasn't her man, he was someone else's. But right now, walking along the street with Max by her side made her realize once again how much she'd missed him.

She was glad she'd refreshed herself before heading out on her walk. She hadn't really given it a second thought when she pulled on some clothes from the clean pile of laundry, and was grateful that what she'd chosen was halfway decent. The short jean skirt was very short, and she wouldn't be bending over anytime soon. Her turquoise toenails matched the sparkly, insanely high sandals she wore. She loved shoes and in fact, when she'd put them on earlier, an idea popped into her mind to change the name of the bakery to We Bake in Heels. It was fun—cool and fresh. She hadn't considered changing the name earlier, but the thought excited her.

Even the fuchsia tank top she wore had blue prisms scattered across the front in the shape of a flower and it caught the sun nicely. The rich color heightened her newly acquired tan and streaked-blonde curls, making her feel summery. Kara sighed, happy to be out and about in the bustle of the crowd with this sexy guy at her side.

"When were you here last?" he asked. "Before Gram's... funeral, I mean."

A lump formed in her throat and she swallowed, looking up at him. "A while ago."

The expression reflected in Max's gaze was sad, as if his feelings were hurt.

"It was hard, Max. Gram died so suddenly and I didn't really want to socialize. There wasn't a whole lot of time to stay and visit. You know, with work and all."

She couldn't tell him how often she'd picked up the phone and dialed his number just to hear his voice, but was never able to complete the call. The last thing she'd wanted to do was cause any more strife or conflict in his life by opening old wounds.

But, you never forgot your first love. Your first lover. The love never faded. She had a secret place in her heart where she treasured the memories they'd made. They were adults now, and more responsible, mature--plus he was married.

Leaving the way she had after Gram's private funeral had made sense at the time.

Max took her hand. "Well, you could--no, you should've called anyway. C'mon, let's get a glass of wine."

"Really?"

"What?" He looked perplexed.

"Max, don't you have your own wine?" She tugged his hand as if trying to make a point.

"Sure. But that doesn't mean I can't buy my own wine or taste another." He pulled her along through the crowd.

She smiled. "Okay, you read my thoughts. I'd planned to stop for a glass anyway." Good thing he couldn't read them all!

He took her bag and ushered her around to head back the way they'd come. A short walk later, he steered her onto a patio behind a wonderful wall of flowers. It was delightfully shaded with green and red market umbrellas and a tree arched over the patio shading the patrons under its wide branches. At first glance it didn't look as though there were any seats available. "Oh, there's one." Kara pointed to a small table tucked behind a fountain. Max guided her with his hand hovering at her waist.

It was as if he touched her. The electricity between them almost crackled and she glanced at him to see if he felt it, too. Their eyes met and he smiled, revealing the dimple she adored. Oh, yeah, she was pretty sure he felt it, too, and butterflies took flight in her belly. The ache between her thighs deepened...

He held the chair while she sat. His fingers lightly stroked the bare flesh of her shoulder, and goose bumps rose up on her arms and her nipples hardened.

Kara needed to distract herself and glanced around for something other than Max to focus on. She was impressed by how this old pizza place had been turned into a hopping wine bar. The second-floor patio was packed and had a roof structure with wooden beams spanning out over the seats. She decided to check out the kitchen later--all in the name of research, of course.

"Are you hungry?" She asked him as he sat.

"Mm. Actually, I'm starved." She could have sworn the look he gave her meant starved but not for food. "Let me order."

Her gaze roamed over his features while he studied the menu. Memories of their intimate times together as teenagers made her belly tumble. They'd explored each other, learning everything they could. Experimenting sexually, which they thought was very adult of them. She let out a breath through pursed lips. They faced each other. She was flushed and fidgeted in the chair.

"What?" Max leaned closer to her.

"Oh, I was just taking a walk down memory lane," she said. Her voice faltered. He'd known her well enough when they were younger to know when she was turned on.

"What kind of walk were you on?" he asked in a low voice.

He knew what she was thinking. Her cheeks flamed but she didn't look away.

"Max," she said, her voice almost a whisper. He'd always been able to read her like a book.

He gave her slow wink before returning his attention to the menu.

She liked sitting here, especially with Max. *But he's married,* Kara reminded herself. She decided not to think about that right now and simply enjoy their time together.

A young, harried server wove his way toward them through the crowded tables. She let Max order, not paying attention. Kara sighed and sat back in the chair, her bag tucked between her feet. For the first time in quite a while, she was relaxed and enjoyed the natural high. It'd been a long time since she'd felt this content.

"How's the reno coming?" Max asked.

"Really good. We're almost done. Everything's turning out exactly like I wanted."

"And if I know you, you had everything organized to a T. You didn't need any help?"

"We have it all under control, plus I didn't want to bother you." She crossed her legs, letting her bag lean against her calf.

"It would've been no bother." The sincerity in his gaze made her feel guilty for not asking him, and she felt a pang at the missed opportunity. Yet being here with him now made up for the days spent without him.

The waiter arrived with their drinks and set the slender glasses before them. "Ice wine? Now?" Kara asked.

"Sure, why not?" He lifted the glass and swirled it, watching the golden liquid twirl around and cling to the sides with its richness. He sniffed and closed his eyes. "Nectar of the gods." Then he sipped.

Kara did the same and was surprised by the sweet burst of flavor on her tongue. "Oh, my goodness! This is fabulous. It's been ages since I've had any." The chilled wine raced down her throat and settled in tingly warmth in her belly, sparking her banked arousal to a higher temperature.

"Good, isn't it?" Max looked at her over the rim of his glass. "Ice wine is such a happy accident much like champagne was."

"Mm, better than good. It's the best I've tasted." She took another sip. "What winery?"

He sipped again and paused for a beat. "Mine."

She couldn't have been more surprised. "Yours?" She didn't know what to say.

"Yep, mine," he said proudly.

"Wow, Max, this is really good." She took another sip, appreciating it in a whole new way. "We need to talk some business then."

He sat back and laughed. "I thought you'd never ask."

The afternoon crept leisurely by and Kara enjoyed a mellow languor she hadn't experienced in such a long time. Sure, it was the wine and the company, but this little bit of patio time in her hometown was the best medicine.

Max ordered a scrumptious antipasto plate and slid his chair around the table beside her so they could share. Their knees touched, sending little shock waves of desire along her nerve endings to settle between her thighs, keeping her arousal at a pleasant hum. She didn't move her leg and he didn't move his.

Their connection continued to grow like a live wire sparking between them. She wondered if he was as turned-on as she was. And when he glanced at her, she knew. The look in his eyes that drove her to distraction as a teenage girl was reflected in his gaze. A little shiver of delight ran down her spine.

She kept glancing at him, unable to take her eyes off him. They had since moved to a nice Pinot Grigio rather than the ice wine and both glasses now sat empty, begging to be filled. She wondered if it was wise to order more. But she longed to continue sitting here with him, sipping wine, people-watching and being enveloped in the intoxicating scent of Max and the flowers. Kara was captivated by him all over again.

He draped his arm across the back of her chair in a casual movement and her heart did a little jump when his thumb stroked her bare shoulder. The air between them sizzled and she decided the decision had been taken from her. She'd stay. Here, with him, and she'd let jazzy tunes from the hidden speakers wrap them in contentment.

"So, you liked the wine, eh?" His voice held a new and sultry tone.

"Yes, it was very nice. I should do a sweets night featuring your ice wine." She leaned in to him slightly, just enough for her shoulder to brush his.

"I like that idea."

"Good. Me, too." Kara needed to bring up something important, but didn't know how and was afraid it would shatter the fragile ease that was developing between them. But she had to for her own peace of mine. Things were getting heated and she had to find out one way or another.

She looked him dead in the eye, searching and watching for a reaction.

"Max. A-are you still marr..." He shook his head and Kara let the word trail away.

Relief flooded through her and she could have jumped for joy. But she only smiled and nodded, not wanting to press it further right now. When he was ready, she knew he'd share the details with her. Time for that later. The fact that he was no longer married was all she needed to know.

He gazed at her intently and raised his eyebrows. "Do you want to know why?"

This time Kara shook her head and wagged her finger back and forth. "Not really. At least right now. I just needed to know your, um, situation."

He sat back and smiled. "Don't want be the other woman, eh?"

Kara laughed and covered her mouth with her fingers, a little embarrassed. "No, definitely not on my bucket list!"

She also felt a little ashamed of being so thrilled by the news that he wasn't married. Divorce was never easy.

The rest of the afternoon fell to mindless, comfortable banter and Kara's contentment grew. The stress and hectic days prior began to fade away and she relaxed more as the afternoon wore on.

Her mind began to wander. What would come next? How would they part? Should she ask him to come back to her patio and open another bottle of wine? She remembered she didn't have anything so they'd have to pick some up. Worry furrowed her brow and she jumped when his hand rested on her shoulder. His fingers traced up the column of her throat and pushed into the curls at her nape, massaging gently. The movement chased the worry from her.

"Mm, that feels lovely." Kara smiled and faced him. She shivered in delight and he chuckled at her involuntary reaction.

"Cold?"

She shook her head and without a second thought leaned toward him. He encouraged her with a gentle tug. She was lost in his eyes and just before their lips met, Kara's eyelids fluttered closed.

Her breath caught when he kissed her—chaste and gentle, but with an underlying power she longed to unleash. Kara craved it and kissed him back, opening her mouth to dart her tongue out and taste his. He met her with a sudden ferocity that liquefied her insides. She was helpless to resist him, her muscles slack and weak. If he didn't have his arm around her, she would have dissolved into a puddle of passion at his feet.

Kara forgot where they were. All sense of place and time had vanished. Her hand crept up to the back of his neck and her fingers played with his hair. Sound faded and Kara was only aware of him, nothing else. She sensed the sexual tension building in him and knew they should slow down before they embarrassed themselves in public. But she couldn't stop and moved closer to him, needing the feel of his body next to hers.

The sharp ring and vibrating buzz of her cell phone on the metal table pierced the moment and she jolted away, almost panting. Kara couldn't catch her breath and fumbled to grab the phone. It was the bakery number.

"Hel—hello." She cleared the roughness from her throat and glanced at Max, who was flushed and watching her intently. His dark gaze her made her promises she wanted him to keep. Kara looked away to try to rebalance herself. "Um, hello?"

"Hi, Kara." It was Jilly, one of her co-op students. "Hey, are you all right?"

"Uh, sure. Why?"

"You sound kinda weird."

Weird? No, just incredibly horny. "What do you need?" she asked a little too harshly and immediately regretted it.

"Oh, the health inspector is here."

"What? Holy shit, I completely forgot." Kara's passion was extinguished as if a bucket of cold water had been sloshed on her. "I'll be right there."

She quickly gathered her bags and turned to Max. "I gotta go. Totally forgot an appointment." She placed her palm on his cheek. "Thank you, it was a great afternoon."

She stood and ignored the curious looks from the other patrons and dashed from the patio. As she rounded the wall of flowers, she glanced over her shoulder at Max. He leaned comfortably in his seat, his arm once again draped across the back of the chair she'd been sitting in. He winked and smiled at her.

Holy crap.

That one simple and utterly sexy look nearly made her stumble. How could she possibly concentrate on a boring old health inspector now?

6

———————

Everything was ready. The bakery passed all tests with flying colors, and Kara was granted a liquor license. She was pleased it had all came together in time for the August Civic Holiday weekend. Her goal was to open by that weekend so she could catch the remainder of the summer tourist season to get a solid foundation as they headed into fall.

She stood with her hands on her hips and observed the room with pride. The We Bake in Heels makeover had turned out to be even more successful than she could have imagined. The combination of antiques and keeping the old world charm, blended perfectly with the new contemporary touch blended perfectly.

Gram had been meticulous about staying up to date on most things, and she'd kept all her old and antiquated baking tools. Kara would use some of them, but had refreshed the kitchen in order to help with the mass production she planned later on.

Kara wandered over to the honey-gold, aged maple shelves that lined the back wall. Resting her hand on the wood, which was warm beneath her palm, she imagined she could feel the history of the bakery. It was a fanciful notion, but she tried nonetheless, and memories running around the shop as a child, standing on a stool beside her gram at the marble worktop in the kitchen or taking orders from customers she could barely see behind the counter brought tears to her eyes.

She allowed herself a moment of melancholy. Carefully storing the memories away, Kara appreciated the newly installed glass doors that fit perfectly with the décor and the cabinets showcasing the antique pieces no longer suitable for use. She'd found some real treasures stored away and placed them in the display, along with pictures of Gram from the old days. Kara used the numerous old butter and cheese boxes she'd found stashed in the storage area as shelves and holders for a variety of items that needed a home. The carefully placed lighting highlighted her treasures behind the glass. Treasures worth more than gold to her.

Kara collapsed into a deep leather chair and curled her legs under her. This corner inside the front door to the left created a perfect little cozy alcove for people to rest away from the hubbub and sip the bevvy of their choice, using free Wi-Fi.

She placed her cup on the battered old oak table she'd hauled down from the living room upstairs. Its scarred and hardened surface gave further antique authenticity to the decor of the shop. She dropped her notebook on the table beside her drink and stretched her arms over her head. Drawing in a big breath, trying to get the kinks out of her back.

Leaning forward she grabbed her book, flipped it open and ran her finger down the list of foods she put on the menu. It was just right. Originally she'd decided to keep it simple and then add a new item each week, but she was rethinking it. She also wanted to launch a new food treat weekly, hoping it would create a buzz and keep people coming back to see what new tasty treat was on the menu.

She would offer sweet treats, of course, like tarts and squares, pastries, croissants, all with a touch of what she'd learned in France, and there would be savory foods, too, suitable for lunch. She didn't want We Bake in Heels to be a sandwich bar, so there wouldn't be any on the menu. She was still deciding about an International Night with higher-end finger foods from places she'd visited and pairing that with wine tasting evenings.

Kara sipped the latte she'd made for herself, glad she'd bought the fancy machine even though it had cost a small fortune. Her bank account cried a little, but was a necessity if she wanted to compete and bring a little bit of Europe to Old Town.

She was happy. Kara hadn't realized how empty she'd felt until now. She'd floated from one day to the next all these years, going wherever the jobs took her and not paying any mind to where that was...except now, that she'd come home.

Not until she made the decision to come home after Gram's death did she understand how she'd let herself drift along the days of her life as if she were a dandelion on the breeze, unsure where she'd land.

She had lived in Paris, South of France, London and Italy with little jaunts to Spain and Greece, soaking up what she could learn from the local chefs and honing her craft. It had been wonderful, but she was aware of a gnawing empty space deep inside her. Something was missing. Of course, she'd learned a lot, been exposed to some pretty spectacular events and met some impressive people, but home is home and she began to miss it. Life, for the first time in a long time, felt settled, complete.

There was only one dark cloud in her blue sky. Max. They hadn't seen each other since last week. And the kiss...

She thought about him a lot. He intruded into her thoughts at the most inopportune moments, usually when she needed to focus. Getting him out of her head wasn't working out all that well. It would have been far easier to throw her hands in the air and say *Well, shit, let's just take a moment and relive our romantic afternoon and that kiss.* But doing that would only have made her long for the real thing.

He hadn't come by but had called and texted a couple of times. They were playing phone tag. She pushed her cell around on the table. She'd been the last to text and hadn't heard back from him yet.

What the heck.

Kara dialed his number and it went to voice mail, the message stating that he was out of the country and would reply to all calls upon his return. Well, at least that explained why she hadn't heard from him. She didn't leave a message.

She would have to let their lovely afternoon and that kiss carry her through the days and into the lonely nights until she saw him again. Which, she hoped, would be very soon.

7

———

Max walked between the rows of grapes, inhaling the smells of the earth, air, grass recently cut and admired the ripening fruit on the vines. He stood among the plants fanning for acres on either side of him, the rows rigid in their perfection. He paused at a small grove, fenced off, where the oldest trees on the property stood. Their branches were gnarly and twisted with age, but they still produced the most delicious apples. As long as he could remember, the family would come out to pick the apples and sell them at their fruit stand in the fall. They were known for them. Tolman Sweet, a Heritage apple dating back to the late 1700s. He wasn't sure how they got here or when they were planted, since the orchard was already here when his family purchased the land over one hundred years ago.

The family also grew tender fruit--peaches, cherries and nectarines. There was nothing like fresh Niagara fruit. The sun was bright today and Max raised his hand to shield his eyes and took in the land. All theirs. The Stones'. He'd been careful to preserve the Heritage trees, and he sent a silent thank you back through the years to the original home-steaders.

The move made more than twenty-five years ago to switch from a seasonal roadside fruit vendor to planting grape vines was the best decision his family had made. Mainly at his insistence. Their vineyard had flourished and many of their wines received awards internationally as well as at home in Canada.

Drawing in a deep breath, he turned his attention to the vines. Assessing them with a critical and educated eye. Everything was ripening on schedule and all the indications were that it would be another bumper crop. If the weather cooperated, they'd be in good shape. He plucked an immature fruit, popped it between his lips and pushed his tongue against the grape. His mouth exploded with tart flavor. He cupped a bunch of the grapes and lifted carefully, assessing the weight.

He hadn't had a chance to call Kara since getting back from his business trip yesterday. Their afternoon at the wine bar stayed with him like a sweet memory and their kiss hadn't satiated his need for her, only made it more intense. He knew she was as busy as he was. It wouldn't be fair to swoop down on her and whisk her off to bed without a little bit of courting first. He longed to touch her, taste her, to explore her body and make love to her. But his timing was off. He had all kinds of conference calls and meetings here, in Toronto the States and a few in Europe.

He wished he could blow off some of the meetings, but they were too important to the business. Max decided he would call her tonight before taking off again. He hoped they'd be able to connect this time.

He wandered through the vineyard, and his thoughts continued to revolve around Kara. God, she looked good.

And after seeing her for the first time in so many years, he realized how much he'd missed her. But why she'd left still needed to be answered. They had grown up together, went to the same school, attended the same birthday parties. Then at fifteen, they discovered each other in a different way, becoming inseparable. He smiled, remembering the fun times in the bakery eating fresh pastries on the patio and picnicking down by the river. They sat for hours talking about their future, what they wanted to do when they grew up and even about getting married. It seemed so easy and clear back then, not at all complicated. Until she disappeared. Just like that. Poof, gone.

His lips tightened, the pain not easy to forget. At the time, he thought his heart had been ripped out and as the old saying goes, you don't know what you've got till it's gone. His family didn't seem to care much about it or what he went through. But looking back, they hadn't really embraced Kara, especially his mother, making things very awkward for them as a couple. His father had been too wrapped up in the business to notice much of what went on. His intensity led to an early heart attack, leaving Max to abandon his ideas of university, traveling to Italy and France for further oenology and viticulture education.

He recognized now how easily influenced he and Kara had been by the adults around them. Max kicked a rock, then leaned down to pick it up. He'd been a wreck when she hadn't answered his calls. And Gram had only said that she was sorry, but Kara had left...

His mother said it was for the best and refused to talk to him about Kara after that. Gram had been different, though —he could tell she truly was sorry. She'd been gentle with him every time he stopped by the bakery to find out if there was any news of Kara. He always left disappointed that she hadn't sent a message for him.

He'd almost gone to France after her, but when his father died he couldn't. He needed to run the place and his mother made no bones about how foolish it would be to chase after someone who had no interest in him and began to push another girl on him. Patricia Howe. Her family had the neighboring farm, but he kept a wide berth from her and his mother's meddling. He'd stayed, and his uncle had come to live with them and help out.

Max got reckless for a while, feeling the need to rebel against the expectations placed on him and his loss of freedom. But his cavalier behavior caught up with him and came home to roost when Caroline, another girl he grew up with, tricked him into marrying her, claiming she was pregnant. His mother wasn't thrilled, preferring Patricia, but encouraged the match since Caroline also came from a wealthy family and the Stones could benefit from the connection. Max learned a few very valuable lessons at a young age when they separated shortly after the discovery that she'd faked the pregnancy. After the legal battles were over and their business remained intact, Max turned all his attention to the vineyard.

He kicked another rock along the row, remembering those troubled years, and felt the familiar ache in his heart.

And Kara, well, she'd just faded into the past like a distant memory. His anger with her eventually dissipated over the years turned into satisfying memories. He knew she'd completed a Cordon Bleu cooking school course in Paris and traveled around Europe, but had no idea when or if she'd be back.

He picked up the stone he'd been kicking and dropped it into a rock pile at the end of the row. Max pulled the baseball cap lower over his eyes to shield them from the sun and mounted the stairs to the sprawling wraparound veranda of the house he'd built. It sat on a rise overlooking the vineyards, shaded by wonderful mature trees. The house he grew up in was now the offices and attached to the shop by this covered deck. He gazed across his land again and felt a strong sense of pride. He'd come a long way and had an exciting future ahead of him. Only he didn't want to spend it alone. There was a hole in him that no amount of business success could fill.

Kara was still in his blood. Nor could he forget the silky feel of her skin or her enthusiastic response to him when they kissed last week--or anything about her for that matter.

Nothing would help ease his desire for her. His cock grew heavy as he recalled their passionate nights down by the river's edge, where they'd first made love and become more adventurous together. Her appetite for sex matched his, something he hadn't found since and he certainly had tried. Max groaned and the tightening in his groin didn't help matters. It wasn't just sexual. Oh yeah, he desired her, but there was more. She held a very special place in his heart.

Now that she'd returned, his ghostly memory was no longer hazy. She was real, alive and here. And the memories of Kara and his teenage love for her began to ripen like the grapes on his vines after the rain and under the sun. He wanted her back.

8

———

A soft summer breeze blew in the open second-floor windows. The scent of roses climbing the front wall of the bakery blended deliciously with scents of the pastries baking in the ovens below. We Bake in Heels would be open to the public for the first time since Gram had died, and under a new name. A nervous stomach kept Kara from eating anything, even though she was starved. It didn't matter how delectable everything smelled, she couldn't put anything past her lips just yet. Not even a coffee.

She checked her watch. Ten more minutes. "Oh, God. Why am I so nervous?"

Because you don't want to fail, that's why. Could she live up to Gram's reputation? She heard laughter and shuffling around downstairs. The culinary baking students she'd hired from the college were busy and they seemed to enjoy the steady panic that had consumed the kitchen for the past week. Part of their program was to acquire co-op training hours, and she needed the help. Thank the Lord for Niagara College so close by. Kara took a deep breath and made her way down the back stairs. Jilly and Shane looked up from organizing cases of baked goods and smiled at her.

"Are you ready?" she asked.

They both nodded, excitement written all over their faces. "It's going to be great," Shane assured Kara. He was a giant, well over six foot three, blond and blue-eyed with a passion for cooking and baking that rivaled hers. She was glad to have found him.

Jilly, a friend and fellow student of Shane's, had her braided hair pulled neatly back beneath a red-and-white kerchief. She was a unique individual, and never had Kara seen such a variety of tattoos and piercings. Jilly was dedicated and very creative.

"Well, almost time, and looks like you both have it all under control." Kara hesitated at the counter and took a deep breath before she walked to the front of the shop. She glanced above the counter at the antique clock she'd found in the storage room. Four minutes. She took in all the wonderful plants and flower arrangements sent by her neighboring businesses, welcoming and wishing her the best. She was so pleased to receive their warm greetings, she'd sent them thank-you plates loaded with samples of what she would be offering in the bakery.

"Okay, time to open the door." Kara gave a quick glance around. Everything was organized and clean, with extra inventory waiting to be brought front of house when needed.

The shop itself thrilled her. It was perfect, and she had absolutely no complaints about the restoration. She had delighted in all the little trinkets she'd found tucked away, which were now on display. She'd even found a real treasure, a small signed original Trisha Romance painting, which Kara had hung in a prominent place on the wall. How on earth Gram had managed to score an original painting by Trisha Romance was beyond her. But it was definitely an honor to have it in the shop, especially since her gallery was just around the corner.

The day was going to be hot and Kara decided to run the air conditioner on low so it would help keep heat out of the store, while the open windows allowed the smell of baked goods to waft onto the street. Kara refused to think about the power cost and justified the expense, which was worth it to create a presence and keep customers comfortable.

She pulled open the heavy wooden door and propped an old crock full of summer blooms in front of it, then turned Gram's old hand-painted sign around. *Open.*

Kara stepped outside to unwind the awning and was shocked to see people already sitting at the iron patio tables waiting for the shop to open.

"Good morning! Please, come inside."

A chorus of "good mornings" greeted her, and Kara stood aside while the customers filed through the door. She glanced up at the old sign. The peeling paint had been carefully stripped away to reveal the original letters underneath. She'd decided to keep the original sign in honor of Gram. The new large one shaped like a stiletto shoe was fastened to the building beside the door and another one swayed on an iron post closer to the sidewalk.

"This is for you, Gram," she whispered and when tears filled her eyes, she didn't care.

Kara sighed and the flutter of happiness in her belly banished all the anxiety she'd felt earlier this morning. People had come. It was going to be a great day.

And it was. The day streaked by with barely a chance for

them to catch their breath until a lull came around two-thirty. Kara touched Shane on the arm. "Why don't you and Jilly take a break while you can?"

He glanced at the door. "Are you sure?"

"Yes, go. If anyone comes in, I can handle it. Grab something to eat and drink and go rest your feet out on the patio."

She watched them select a few pastries and a drink, then collapse in a shady spot out front.

Excitement still bubbled in her and Kara coasted on a natural high. She felt great! The turnout had been huge and they'd restocked the cases several times. After a quick inventory check she knew there would be just enough to carry them until closing, and if they were lucky, a few left-over treats. She got a damp cloth and wiped down the counters and café tables at the internet bar. No one had brought a laptop yet, but she wasn't concerned. People expressed surprise that it was offered, assuring her the next time they came, they'd bring their computers. Once she'd tidied everything up, Kara pulled a bottle of sparkling water from the cooler behind the counter. She poured a glass and dropped in a sliver of lime. She finished her drink in a long swallow and poured another one. Sipping while she turned around, Kara nearly choked when she saw Max standing there with a big grin on his face.

"Hi! Oh, you surprised me." Damn, he looked good, and she quickly swept a drop of water from her lips.

"Hey, Kara. I couldn't let your opening day go by without a visit." He presented her with a huge basket of fresh herbs, gathered in bunches and a few in pretty pots.

Kara laughed. "Oh, Max, how thoughtful." She accepted them across the counter and placed the rectangular basket on the deep window ledge. "I'm glad you came. What would you like?"

"How about you pick me a sampling of your favorites?"

She pushed flyaway curls off her brow and hoped her mascara wasn't smudged too badly. She folded a large takeout box together.

"All right then. Let's see."

She picked a number of things she knew he liked and added some of her own favorites— butter tarts, spanakopita, cheese puffs, cream puffs, mini croissants, upside-down puff savories and a few other delectable treats. Then she chose the biggest, flakiest chocolate croissant for him, knowing it was his longtime favorite. She handed the package over the counter to him.

"You remembered." The husky tone in his voice sent thrills of delight along her flesh.

"How could I forget? The croissant will be the best you've ever tasted. Remember, I've had formal training in the art of French delights, er, pastry."

He laughed out loud and the deep timbre warmed her heart.

"How much?" Max reached his free hand into his pocket.

"Don't be ridiculous! I'm not going to charge you." Kara waved her hand, dismissing the idea.

"I insist on paying." He had his wallet out.

"And I won't take any money from you. My treat." Then she gave him a devilish smile. "Remember the rooster?"

For a moment he looked perplexed and then laughed again. "Okay, but you're spoiling me."

"I know." She smiled, enjoying their flirtation.

"Has it been busy?"

"Oof, from the minute we opened the door until now. I

shooed them outside to take a rest." She nodded to Shane and Jilly sitting in the shade.

"I'm glad." His face was earnest. "It's good to see the doors open at Fingertips again, Kara. But what's with the new sign out front?"

She shivered, loving how her name rolled off his tongue. "The idea struck me a while ago. I love to bake and shoes are my weakness, so I combined the two. Do you like it?"

He nodded. "I do. It's original."

"I wish I'd done it long ago. When Gram was still alive." Her heart pained. "If only I'd come home sooner."

"Why didn't you?"

Kara didn't expect his forthright question, assuming he'd smooth it over so she didn't feel bad.

"Well, um, Max…" She paused, trying to think of what to say. How could she explain the reason she'd left, and not hurt him? "Now really isn't the time."

"When will it be the right time, Kara?" She detected a slightly hard edge in his tone.

"I don't know, but please, can we drop it for now?"

She wanted to avoid the pain she saw in his eyes, but didn't look away and forced herself to keep his gaze. She would tell him eventually. But not now. "Max—"

She was interrupted by laughter when Shane and Jilly burst through the door. "Get ready, Kara, there's a crowd coming!" Shane's voice boomed out. He saw Max and hesitated. "Oh sorry, man, didn't mean to interrupt."

"No worries." He reached his hand out. "Max. I'm an old friend of Kara's."

"Shane." He shook Max's hand.

Max turned to Kara, but a crowd burst through the door and swarmed into the bakery before either could say anything further. Their private moment was gone.

She smiled and shrugged her shoulders at him as he was shuffled to the back of the crowd. He touched his fingertips to his brow and returned her smile, then walked out her front door. Even though the shop was brimming with people, it felt very empty with him gone and she tried to catch a glimpse of him through the window.

9

Kara collapsed onto the lounge chair at the end of the day. The deck behind the bakery was nicely shaded and she groaned with delight, toeing off her shoes. Her feet ached, she was exhausted and starving, but felt fantastic. Today had exceeded her expectations tenfold and there were barely any leftovers, which meant an early rise tomorrow to get baking. She groaned thinking about crawling out of bed at 4 a.m. Thank God she had the students to help.

Dusk fell quickly, and the fresh smell of the lake drifted on the sultry summer breeze. It shook the leaves over-hanging the second-floor deck. The rooster chime Max had given her tinkled in the branches and birds tweeted their good night to the world.

She loved her oasis. After the college students lent their creative hands to creating a comfy ambience, she'd snagged a few plants from the overflowing front patio and lugged them up here.

Mini lights along the railing, through the potted flowers

and dangling from the ancient branches spread over the deck, twinkled like fireflies. The students had done a great job, and Kara loved cozy patio furniture, outdoor cushions and strategically placed speakers so the music seemed to float on the air.

A small patio size cast iron fireplace was ready to create the ambiance of a bonfire. This was her sanctuary, where she could retreat and escape. A little fountain gurgled in the corner, helping to drown out the sounds. She loved it.

What I wouldn't give for a glass of wine.

It was the only thing that hadn't made its way onto her very comprehensive shopping list. Shocking, considering she lived in wine country. Kara longed for a crisp glass of rosé and was thrilled to discover that wines from one of her favorite South of France vineyards in Languedoc were available here. She made a mental note to get a box of the Cote des Roses.

She stretched out, wiggling her toes. A foot massage would be divine right about now and would go so well with a glass of wine. She had neither.

The jangle of the old cowbell that hung at the back door startled her. She wasn't expecting anyone and wanted to bark at the intruder to go away. Instead, she swung her legs off the lounge, tiptoed to the railing and peeked down through the canopy of leaves.

Max!

She snapped up straight and her hand flew to her mouth. She stepped forward again just in time to watch him give the rope a good yank. Did she want him to go away? She was tired and badly needed sleep and a shower, but she didn't have the heart to send him along. Kara waited a minute or two to see what he's do. Through the green veil, she saw him take a couple of steps back and peer through the branches at her.

"Kara. I know you're up there. Answer the door!"

10

───────

S he couldn't hide from him.

"What are you doing here, Max?" She cringed, realizing she sounded a little bitchy and didn't mean to.

"I'm here to celebrate."

She stepped forward and leaned over the railing, looking down again, curiosity getting the better of her. "What are you celebrating?"

"Not me, you!"

"Me? What are you talking about?"

"Kara, are you playing dumb? Open the door and let me in."

She realized that Max at her door topped off the day with perfection. Even in her exhausted state, she was glad he'd come.

"Hang on a sec, I'll be right down." Kara dashed into the bathroom. She looked a wreck after the long day and needed a major repair job, but she didn't have time. She wiped a cold facecloth over her flushed skin and under the light tank top she'd changed into, freshening up the girls, then dabbed a dash of perfume behind her ears and between her breasts. She smoothed her hands over her shorts. All this in under a minute. She skipped down the stairs, feeling light-footed and happy. Her Max was here.

He closed the door behind him and locked it. Turning around he waggled his eyebrows at her. Kara laughed. He'd always been able to make her laugh.

The old familiar languor flowed through her veins and she would have walked right into his arms had he not handed her a couple bottles of wine, then rummaged in the drawers.

"What are you looking for?" She held the bottles and read the labels. He's brought his own wine.

"An opener."

His presence filled the room. His being here was as normal as the sun rising each day. He'd–they'd–grown up here and now all these years later, here they were back together. Kara's heart did a little dance.

"Third drawer." It all felt so right. She feasted her eyes on him, watching every move he made. Of course, her thoughts ran to the risqué with him so close to her, and she was so totally absorbed watching him, that he scared the crap out of her when he shouted.

"Aha!" He smiled and raised his hand, holding the corkscrew as if it were a trophy, and took a bottle from her.

Kara returned the smile and enjoyed the vision of him, loving the way the muscles in his forearms flexed with his effortless movements as he twisted the screw into the cork and flicked it out with a pop. It didn't matter if she was expecting the sound, it never failed to startle her. Fireworks did the same thing.

"Scared ya, huh?" He laughed.

"Did not."

"Oh, yeah? I remember how easy you startle." He held up the bottle. "Glasses?"

What house in a wine region would be complete without a full set of wineglasses? Kara's place was no different. A wonderful selection of old goblets sat behind the white-paned glass doors of one of the kitchen cupboards. Kara removed two and held them to the light, inspecting for spots. Satisfied, she set them before Max on the marble counter waiting for the delicious nectar. He handled the bottle carefully, cradling it in his palm and tipping it enough for a perfect pour into the goblet. He ended with an expert twist to catch the final drip.

Max held a glass out to her and her hand tingled when their fingers touched. The sensation rolled in waves across her body and she shivered in delight. He hesitated a brief moment and looked deep into her eyes. She couldn't look away and her belly tumbled over with pleasure. He let his finger stay next to hers longer than necessary before raising the glass to toast.

Oh, God, what was happening?

Kara barely heard his words. He'd succeeded in distracting her completely and she was caught in his spell. Heat raced along her veins and settled in aching need between her thighs. Her nipples hardened and rose against the light tank top. She felt the urge to cover them, but didn't and stood waiting to see if he noticed.

"To your grand opening and..." His looked down and she smiled. He'd noticed. His voice faded away and all she heard was the rushing of blood in her ears. His eyes rose back up and met hers.

She wanted to kiss him.

Badly.

She craved the heat of his mouth on hers, his tongue

probing and encouraging hers to meet his. Kara automatically raised her glass to clink with his when he held it up. She expertly swirled the nectar in the goblet, it was a lovely Rose and held it under her nose to inhale the bouquet. Outstanding.

She sipped, and its heat slipped down her throat. Warmth radiated out, mixing perfectly with her arousal, heightening her desire for him. Now she really wanted to do more than just kiss and drifted off into a fantasy world of the two of them together. She could almost feel his touch, her imagination was so vivid.

"Kara? Where did you go? Lost you there for a bit." She zoned back in on him, in an even higher state of excitement.

Kara took another sip and stepped toward him. She'd be damned if she was going to wait any longer. Time for her to take charge.

She circled one arm around his neck and pulled his head lower, watching the emotions play across his face. For a moment she thought he'd pull away, but he didn't. He set his glass down and grabbed her roughly. He yanked her against his chest and groaned when her breasts pressed up against him. She exploded into a livewire of heightened nerve endings, and if he didn't have her in such a tight grip she wouldn't have been able to stand.

His kiss sent her back in time, as if she was a virgin again, not confident or knowing the power of her sexuality. All her lonely nights of fantasizing about being in his arms had become a reality. She fumbled during the kiss. So did he. Their teeth knocked and they grappled as if they needed to get inside each other. But then primal need took over and they found their pace. Max backed her into the marble counter where she was able set her glass down, dimly aware of the clink when it tipped over, spilling the wine across the surface. But she didn't care. His hands ran down her sides and reached around to grip her ass. He squeezed and she sucked in a breath. Kara clung to his shoulders while he overwhelmed her with his kisses and touch.

He lifted her onto the counter, their lips never parting. Max nudged her knees open with his thigh and stood between them, so wonderfully close to her. Kara pulled at the buttons on his shirt and sent them skittering across the floor. She yearned to feel the warmth of his skin next to hers and pushed the fabric off his shoulders. She broke away, breathless from their kiss, and leaned back in awe of his magnificence.

"Oh, I've missed you," she whispered and ran her hands lightly up his tanned arms and over his shoulders. He didn't move, watching her fingers explore his skin. She turned her hands over and the backs of her fingers whispered over the hard planes of his chest, hesitating against his raised nipples. He shuddered when she grazed the sensitive tips.

"Come closer," she ordered and he complied. Kara slipped her hands and legs around him catching him in her embrace.

She pressed her heels against his ass to bring his hardness next to her wet warmth. Their touch through the clothing was electric, as if they were plugged into each other. The thin top she wore was a hindrance and before she could pull it over her head, Max did. She held her arms up, which raised her breasts provocatively higher. He dropped the shirt and it landed in the spilled wine, soaking the fabric.

Her hands in the air, she stilled and closed her eyes when he caressed her arms, then gently cupped her breasts. Delicious shivers rippled along her flesh, her nerve endings stirred until they tingled and no matter where he touched her, with his mouth or hands, Kara was unable to control the quaking of her muscles.

"You're so beautiful. How I've missed you." He leaned down to nuzzle the sensitive tips. "Mm." She leaned forward, giving him better access, and sighed when his lips nibbled along her collarbone. He trailed a path of heat with his tongue and mapped his way to her tight, aching nipples.

"I know what you want." His voice was muffled against her skin.

"Mm, hm." She couldn't form words and didn't bother to try, she was so caught up in his touch. When they were younger, he had a way of taking her outside herself with feeling. Kara lost sense of the world around her and homed in on the sensations he aroused in her and absorbed everything he offered. Light-headed, she was falling, falling into him, absorbed in the glory of his touch, and tears filled her eyes.

He brought her breasts together and pushed her back. When his lips finally closed over a nipple, she could barely stand it. Her mind emptied. Eyes closed she let herself *feel*. So long, so long since she'd experienced such sublime bliss. Oh, how she'd craved him. Kara pushed her fingers into his hair and held him to her.

He suckled her, driving her wild with his mouth. His tongue. She wanted him nearer and wiggled her ass to get closer to him. She hungered to feel his cock and damn, their clothes were in the way!

When she finally felt his hardness tight against her pussy, she grew damp with the anticipation of him sliding inside her. Kara reached between them to undo his pants and her back came flush with the marble. She let out a surprised yelp at the cold, which shocked her like a dash of frigid water.

"Oh, lets…" she murmured. The patio. They should be up there in the oasis she'd so carefully created. It was the perfect setting to rekindle their passion. "Not here on the cold kitchen counter."

He didn't stop and remained fastened to her breast, his other hand down between them to cup her damp heat through her shorts.

"Max, hang on," Kara moaned and pushed at his shoulders.

"What's wrong?" His voice, husky with desire and passion, reached inside and grabbed her heart. He flexed his hips into her. She sucked in a breath at the evidence that he was as turned on as she was. The look in his eyes, his breathing, the tension in his muscles and most evident, the enticing bulge in his jeans. She'd never seen the grown-up Max turned on and desiring her, only the teenage Max. And boy, oh, boy, she liked what she saw. His rawness and pure masculinity made her feel feminine and desired and she loved every minute of it.

Kara reached for him and taking his hand, she placed it between her thighs. He pressed his fingers into her through the cotton fabric. She closed her legs on his hand and clenched her thighs, heightening her sensation and trapping him.

He growled and leaned in, his face close to hers. "Are you trying to drive me insane?"

She put her hand on his chest to halt him. "Not here, big guy. Let's go upstairs." She ran her tongue along his lower lip before leaning back to regard him.

He answered with a predatory grin. Kara slid off the counter, and his hand slipped from between her thighs when she sidled up to him. She welcomed the thrill when his fingers walked over her belly and up to her breast. He grasped it roughly and she moaned. She needed to touch him. Feel the weight of his cock in her hands. She moved her fingers down his belly and under his waistband, going so she could grasp him. They both sucked in a breath.

Kara loved the feel of him in her hand. She gently squeezed his balls and then ran her palm over the hard length of his cock, desperate to free him.

"Come on," she said. "Grab the bottle." He did as ordered and she took the glasses, wiping the spilled wine. He followed her up the back stairs out to the deck.

He glanced around. "Wow, you've made some great changes here. The last I remember, it needed a lot of TLC."

Kara laughed and sat on the lounge, careful to place the glasses on the table beside her. She reclined and brought one heel to rest on the cushion, while the other leg dangled over the side, her legs delectably spread to tempt him.

"You've turned into an exhibitionist?"

"Not to worry, it's very private here." Her voice sounded unrecognizably husky. When his gaze dipped lower, her power soared. It welled up and she welcomed it. Her sexuality had taken a back seat all these years and so she had the urge to explore her wilder side. She never felt quite comfortable enough to let it out, even when it wanted to be unleashed. Here with Max, that was exactly what she felt safe to do...unleash the wild.

Kara thrilled at the look on his face, the intensity in his stance as he watched her run her hands over her belly and up to her breasts. She closed her eyes and imagined they were his and delighted at the delicious desire that grew within her.

"This is what I want you to do to me," she murmured, opening her eyes to see the passion on his face Her skin was soft, and when her hardened nipples pushed against the palms of her hands, she moaned right along with Max.

Her eyelids fluttered and through half-closed lids she watched him. The wine bottle hung limply in one hand and his other reached for the front of his pants and she knew he was holding himself. She smiled, seeing his hand twitch against his cock when she ran her fingers back down over her belly button to slip inside her shorts.

"Holy shit," he murmured and stepped toward her, placing the bottle alongside the glasses on the table.

Kara arched her back and moved her hand lower, feeling her swollen heat. But she needed more. She needed Max and continued to tease both herself and him. She withdrew her hand; the wave of pleasure was incomplete without his touch. She fumbled with the button and zipper, trying to undo them much too quickly. Before she could take the shorts off, he was kneeling on the lounge, pushing her hands aside as he grasped the waistband.

"You're killing me," he growled in a voice hoarse with arousal. "Lift."

Kara did as she was told, raising her butt off the cushion. He pulled the shorts down, slowly revealing her nakedness. At last she was free of clothes. He sat back on his heels and gazed at her nakedness, passion darkening the chocolate color of his eyes.

"Just as I remember...beautiful." He spread his hands over her belly, fanning them out in a feather touch.

"Come here." She lifted her arms to him and he didn't hesitate.

But rather than lie next to her, he knelt at the foot of the lounge and grasped her ankles. She drew in a surprised gasp and relaxed her muscles, waiting to see what he planned next.

His large, tanned hands gently massaged her calf muscles and then he worked on her feet for a few minutes before sliding higher. She sighed at the pleasure trilling along her nerves. He massaged his way up to her knees and smoothed his palm over her flesh. Then he moved up her thighs, stroking and walking his fingers along the taut muscles. Heaven.

She sighed and her muscles quivered as he inched higher. Kara's knees fell open and she lay wanton before him, loving every second of his seduction.

He glanced down at her and licked his lips. Another shiver ran along her limbs and she felt dampness slip from her. She was ready for him. She had to have him inside her now, his thickness widening her and pushing deep, but she forced herself to try to relax, to enjoy his touch and not rush things. But it had been so long!

She watched him crouched between her thighs and a quiver of intensity spread from her sex, radiating out over her body. She was exposed, vulnerable, and she welcomed it. His fingers roamed up to her clit and he brushed them against her swollen lips, tugging gently on her curls.

"Ahh," Kara murmured. Her back arched at the intimacy of his touch and her passion ripened beyond anything she had experienced before. Waves of orgasm hovered so close and she held on to them, not letting them take over yet.

"Max. Now." Kara raised her hips in invitation.

"Just hang on, darling. I'm having fun discovering you again." And his hands continued their trek. Her muscles trembled in his wake as he remapped her, over the gentle rise of her belly and under her breasts.

"Now you're killing me," Kara whispered and turned her face toward the pillow.

"I aim to please." He chuckled and continued to explore.

She nearly jolted upright when the wet heat of his mouth closed over her erect nipple. Kara clutched at his head, not wanting to let him go, and wrapped her legs around him. But he wasn't going anywhere. She heard the evening bird's sweet song as the sultry night air whispered over them, enveloping her in Max's familiar wild and fresh scent. She ran her hands along the corded muscles of his back and down to his hips. Her fingers stumbled over the waistband of his jeans. She had to get them off.

Max nuzzled his way over to her other breast and she was nearly incoherent with desire. Kara unwrapped her legs and quickly undid the fly. She tried to push his pants down, but he leaned over her, so she didn't have the freedom to remove them completely and only managed to get them to his hips. His lips trailed a blaze of heat to her collarbone and along her chin. When he reached her mouth and kissed her, a moan fell from her lips only to be breathed in by him. He cupped her breast and his thumb brushed across the aching peak. She opened her mouth and welcomed the gentle probing of his tongue. Every touch, taste, whisper of his lips set her nerve endings alight as pleasure crackled along her veins and settled in throbbing bliss between her thighs.

"Max, your pants," Kara murmured against his mouth. She raised her feet to hook her toes into the waistband, deliciously bringing her pussy into scorching contact with his cock. He reached down and pushed the jeans & boxers off until he was naked, too, then placed his hands on either side of her head. He steadied himself with ease and rested between her raised knees. Kara welcomed him against her throbbing wetness and maneuvered her hips, to encourage him inside.

He pushed into her and rather than fill her, his cock

skimmed along her swollen lips to nudge against her clitoris. She cried out and he shushed her with a deeper kiss. Kara dug her heels into his ass and pulled him to her, grinding against him. Exquisite pleasure tightened low in her belly and she ached for the brilliant orgasm she knew would come.

She hadn't been this aroused ever, not even when they were teenagers. Max broke away from the kiss and their eyes met. His beloved face hovered so close to hers and emotion swelled within her, swirling the tender and ferocious feelings until she was lost in sensation.

She wanted him to fuck her now. She couldn't wait any longer. Her fingers reached for him and closed around his hard length. She pushed him back and wriggled out from under him. He fell onto his back and lay beneath her on the lounge. Kara's knees braced him and she straddled his thighs, holding him tight. His mature body thrilled her far beyond the teenage boy from so long ago, and she reveled in him.

"You're so gorgeous." She fell over him to run kisses along his chest, lightly covered with dark curls, and ran her hand across his pectoral muscles, which flexed beneath her touch.

"Not so bad yourself." His husky voice was edged with desire.

Max's fingertips pushed into her tangled hair and he leaned up, the muscles in his belly flexed when he buried his face in her curls. "I can't believe you're here and back in my arms. Where you belong." He kissed her neck, up to her earlobe, and suckled on it. "You smell like butter and almonds."

Kara smiled and placed her hand on his cheek, turning him so he faced her. She was almost moved to tears seeing the passion and love in eyes. She knew her love for him was evident and she didn't care. She belonged here, with him. Just as he'd said...

Kara closed the distance between them and touched her lips to his, a kiss that told him more than words could ever say. His arms held her tight and they fused together. She let everything go. All the worry and concern that had been eating at her for so long, gone. Just like that. Even the nasty words his mother had said all those years ago, gone. It was history and she was here in the present, in his arms.

"Lie back," she murmured against his lips and pushed him down. When he was fully reclined, she sat back and stared down at his superb chest, across his muscled belly, hips and the sharp ridge framing the strip of hair that ran from his belly button to the dark curls between his thighs.

That was where her treasure waited. His wonderful cock stood proud. She was also completely exposed, and it was so unbelievably erotic to see their nakedness close together. She took him in her hand, curled her fingers around his erection. She stroked up, around the head and back down. He was wonderfully hard, and she didn't think getting even harder was possible, but he did under her touch and his groan of pleasure spurred her on.

Kara couldn't wait any longer. She ached to feel him inside her and raised her body, balancing over him. With her hands, she guided him to her sex and was about to lower herself when she remembered. "Do you ha—"

Seeming to read her mind, he interrupted. "Pass my jeans."

Kara reached down, picked them up from the deck and handed them to him. He rummaged in a pocket and triumphantly showed her the packet.

"Let me." She took it and tore the wrapping with her

teeth while she continued to stroke him. She held the condom over the tip of his throbbing penis and waited. She smiled when he raised his hips toward her. He wanted this just as much as she did. Kara rolled it down until he was sheathed.

"Now you're ready," she whispered.

"Am I?" He chuckled and grasped her shoulders. Kara's head fell back and Max ran his hands up to the back of her neck and pulled her to him. She held her breath when her breasts pushed against his muscled chest. Erotic heat radiated outward in a rush and returned like ripples on a pond to settle in agonizing, pulsing heat between her thighs. Oh, God.

He shifted below her and moved her until she was beneath him. A surprised "Oh!" burst out of her mouth at the sudden switch of their positions.

"Now you're where I want you." He ran his hands lightly across her collarbone, sending delicious shivers across her flesh. He mesmerized her and she watched the movement of his hands sweep slowly back and forth, raising her arousal to knife-edge sharpness. His cock nestled on her belly and she wiggled her hips, creating a more intimate contact between them. She couldn't tear her gaze away from his fingers as they played with her nipples and plucked them into harder buds. They ached in time with her clitoris, both begging and longing for attention and release.

"So lovely Max murmured before he ducked his head and flicked his tongue across a nipple, then pulled it between his lips. He gently grazed his teeth across the sensitive flesh and ran his hands down her belly to her clit. She arched under him when his fingers found what they sought.

"Ooooooh, Max...please." She squirmed under him,

unable to take much more of his exquisite torture. He pleasured her so deftly Kara's coherent thoughts vanished and when he wedged his knee between her thighs, she needed no encouragement and opened to him, aching to feel his hard and delicious length inside her.

"Now, Max, now!"

This time he listened to her and pushed into her waiting heat, slow and steady. She opened for him, unable to contain her outcry, and raised her hips to meet his thrusts.

"Harder." Her teeth clenched and she encouraged him to lose himself in the wild abandon of the raw sexuality she craved. Kara's fingers gripped his ass and he groaned when her nails dug in. He thrust harder and she met him. Max shifted until he sat on the lounge and positioned her on his lap. She tightened her legs around his hips, holding him deep within her. The angle placed her in perfect alignment with him, every part of them united. Her clit rubbed against his coarse curls, intensifying her stimulation. He filled her completely, and each thrust created delicious pressure against her G-spot.

Incredible tension built like an elastic band being pulled beyond its limit. Kara clutched his shoulders and rode him. He held her tight and safe in his arms and she let everything else go, taking tiny, quick gasps of breath while her vision faded. She clung to him, the intensity of her orgasm catapulting her beyond anything except euphoria. Max silenced her cry of pleasure with his mouth and their lips clung together, each breathing the other's breath.

11

―――

Kara's pussy tightened around him. He couldn't hold back any longer. With one last hard thrust he came. He felt as if he'd been turned inside out--never had he been so overwhelmed by ecstasy. He held her tight while they rode out the long-awaited blissful pinnacle of their orgasms.

He didn't let her go and they slowly came back to reality. Max lowered her onto the lounge and slowly their breathing returned to normal. They didn't move, and after a few minutes, Max disentangled himself from her and rose.

"Be right back." He dropped a tender kiss on her forehead and Kara smiled at him. He looked at her nakedness briefly, then turned, leaving her to snuggle on the cushions. He knew where the bathroom was and made use of it.

It had happened. He'd come over here hoping to share a bottle of wine, with no expectations of making love. She'd been like a starved lioness and he loved it. A happy chuckle came from him and he knew he had a stupid grin on his face, but right now he didn't give a shit. He was here with

Kara. Something he'd never thought would be possible again.

A robe hung on the back of the door. She might need it, so he draped it over his arm. In the hallway he stopped. She'd made some changes to the rooms, mostly bringing things up to date and decorating with her personal items. He sighed. It was wonderful to be back here.

He went downstairs. It wasn't hard to find food in a chef's kitchen and he loaded a plate with some delicious looking grub and trotted back up the stairs to the deck. The sight that greeted him took his breath away.

Kara had switched on the twinkle lights. The golden glow from the hurricane glass shades flickered across the deck, creating a cozy and welcoming ambience. Branches overhead swayed in the night breeze and the fountain gurgled in the corner. But none of that was what stopped his breathing and set his blood on fire again. It was Kara lying on her side, angled perfectly so the candlelight flattered her naked figure. He swallowed and felt his cock stir. She could've been an artist's sculpture, her skin like marble and perfection under the lights.

"Maybe I should hire you to be a waiter." She looked pointedly between his legs. "Dressed like that, you'd definitely bring in the ladies."

He put the plate down on the table and freshened the wine in their glasses. She accepted the one he offered and sipped, her stare heavy on him.

"Anytime, sunshine, just say the word." He leaned down for a kiss before placing the robe beside her, then grabbed his jeans. "Hope you don't mind, but I was starving." He reached for a small pastry, put it into his mouth and chased it with a sip of wine. "I thought you might like your robe, since your clothes are scattered all over the place. It was on the hook in the bathroom."

"Thanks. I'd forgotten how hungry I was, too." She leaned forward to grab something from the plate, seemingly in no rush to put on the robe, sitting with her legs to the side and taking a savory tart.

He watched every move she made. Even the simple act of putting her arms into the sleeves and pulling the edges of the turquoise wrap together was crazy sexy. The edges of the satin clung to her breasts and the enticing gap showcased her cleavage. He caught himself glancing down and thoroughly enjoyed the view. She didn't seem to mind, if her nipples pushing against the fabric were anything to go by.

He settled into the low armchair in front of her and stretched his legs out, propping his bare feet on her lounge. He felt relaxed. "So. What now?"

Kara took a sip of wine. "What do you mean 'what now'? I'm quite happy doing just this." She leaned forward to snag a lamb pop.

Her robe gaped open, exposing the swell of her breasts. She leaned back and closed her eyes, nibbling on the treat, then took another taste of wine. He was still horny. Their one mind-blowing session wasn't nearly enough to satisfy all the years of neglect and frustration without her. But it could all be over in the next few minutes. He knew the risk of asking her, but he had to. He wondered how she'd react. He was also a little worried about his own reaction when she finally told him the reason.

"Kara, why did you leave?" The chimes of the rooster tinkled in a sudden breeze.

S he kept her eyes closed and tried to remain calm, but took a deep breath as her heart kicked into high gear. She knew he'd want answers and she really did owe him an explanation. But damn if his bitch of a mother shouldn't be the one to tell him what she did.

"Have you spoken to Joyce?" She knew her voice sounded harsh and she didn't care. The thought of that woman was infuriating.

He was silent and she opened her eyes to glance at him. His face was unreadable. The cozy ease of the night seemed to hover on the breeze, about to float away.

"What's wrong?" She sat up and closed the robe. Suddenly feeling uncomfortable.

"Kara, I've asked you a few times and you've yet to explain it." His tone made her heart clench with concern. It didn't fit with the mood and afterglow of their lovemaking, and cold tendrils of alarm trickled down her spine. The harshness in his voice startled her and suddenly she felt as if something was really wrong.

"Max, it was such a long time ago." She hoped that maybe after their lovemaking he'd let it drop.

He shook his head. "Kara, why do you want me to talk to my mother?" Kara was unsure what to say. If she said too much or too little, it could ruin everything. The last thing she wanted was to end this wonderful night on a bad note.

She wished he would just let it go; the past was the past and she told him that again.

He ran his fingers through his hair, letting out a frustrated sigh. He looked at her, his eyebrows pulled together. "Maybe so, but I don't understand why you refuse to tell me what made you leave so suddenly. Your words, all I want is your words."

"There were a few reasons. You know I wanted to go to Europe to study, as you did."

"Yes, yes, but we talked about our future together too. Getting married, opening a business."

She could tell he was becoming agitated and panic soured in her belly. She didn't want to tell him his mother had instigated the whole thing. She shivered, remembering the horrible things Joyce had said to her. Even offering her money to leave. Which Kara refused to take, of course. It was offensive to be offered money and told she wasn't good enough for Joyce's son. That he deserved someone of his own "status".

Anger simmered in her chest. How she hated that woman for being the puppeteer who'd changed two lives forever. Kara had never felt comfortable around his mother and she was dying to tell him all the horrible things Joyce had said so many years ago. But she wasn't going to be the one to deliver the news and expose his mother. Joyce had to do it herself.

Clearly what she'd told Kara was a lie. She'd claimed that if Max didn't marry Patricia, the daughter of a neighboring farm family, the Stones might lose their farm. It was an arranged marriage, combining the lands for a bigger empire. How could a girl raised by her grandmother, who owned a bakery, ever be good enough for her son? At the time, when she was a young and impressionable teenager, she believed what adults told her, so why would she think her boyfriend's mother would lie?

He stood and drained his glass, set it down on the table and paced to the railing. Resting his hip against the wood, he faced her, his arms crossed over his chest. The universal body language meaning *back off*. Unapproachable.

Kara sighed and got up. She walked toward him, still

saying nothing but hoping she could somehow salvage the night. She didn't want to burst his bubble about his mom, but the woman was a mean bitch.

She placed her hand on his forearm. "Tell me, what caused your divorce from Patricia?" He blinked, obviously surprised by her question. "What's that got to do with anything?"

"Humor me, Max. Why did you divorce?"

"We shouldn't have gotten married at all." His voice was steel.

"But you did and it was pretty soon after I left, right?"

He didn't answer, so she continued. "Your mom wanted you to marry her. I'd make a bet on that. She came from the right side of the tracks." Kara spoke in a low voice, almost hoping he wouldn't hear her, and glanced up at him from under her brows to watch his reaction. "And I came from the wrong side."

His gaze dropped to her and the intensity of it bored into her. He grabbed her shoulders. "Who told you that?"

"I think you know who did, Max." The pain clutching her heart right now was worse than all those years ago when Joyce had told her she was trash and not suitable for her son. He would make something of himself without Kara, who would only drag him down.

He gripped her shoulders and pulled her to face him. His anger came through in the power of his grip. "Tell me what she said to you."

"Oh, Max. *She* should." Kara continued to keep her voice low, but she tripped over the words, her stress causing bile to rise in her throat. "First, why did you divorce?" Pain clouded his eyes, and she wished she could take it from him. Emotion painted an expression of vulnerability and hurt on his face, and all she wanted was to take his pain away.

She desperately wished she hadn't been one of the people responsible for it. For a brief moment, he looked like the teenage boy she fell in love with and she leaned toward him, but his features hardened.

"I didn't love her." He pushed Kara away and paced across the deck to the rooster in the tree. He took a swat at it. A riotous clanging came from the branches while the rooster danced on its string.

He turned and the words pierced her like an arrow. "I loved *you* then, not her. It was all wrong. I was tricked, and it didn't take long for it to come to a head.

He'd loved her then, but didn't say anything about now.

"Max. I'm sorry—"

"Stop, Kara. I'm pissed that you didn't come to me about it. Instead you ran off. You could've told me! I could have fixed it, we could have been together." Pain stretched his voice.

"But you don't understand!" She didn't want him to be angry with her, and clearly, he was. Damn, and all because of his mother. And maybe a bit of her own pride, too. She'd been stupid to fall for it without checking.

"What I understand is that the women in my life manipulated situations to benefit themselves. I was young and foolish back then. But not now."

Kara shivered. Never had she seen him so angry and it stunned her. To go from their loving just moments earlier to this raw fury was unnerving.

He took his keys out of his jeans pocket and walked to the doorway. "Where are you going?" Panic filled her. He couldn't just leave like this!

He hesitated at the door and gripped the handle. "Kara. Holy shit." He dragged his hands through his hair. "What you're implying changes so much. Trust. We were all about trust back then." A brief flicker of pain in his eyes tore her heart out. "You didn't trust me enough to tell me."

"Don't go." She was close to begging him to stay, but he shook his head and was gone. The back door slammed shut behind him and the throaty roar of his truck shattered the stillness of the night.

Kara leaned over the railing and called after him, but it was too late. Only the spray of gravel hitting the fence from his truck tires was left behind. Kara couldn't keep her tears back any longer. She cried for their lost years, the tenderness they'd shared tonight and what she might have jeopardized for all the tomorrows to come.

She couldn't stop him from leaving. He was angry and felt betrayed. She couldn't change that, but for both their sakes, he needed to know the truth. She had no idea if he'd seek the truth from his mother or if he'd come back to her. Kara could only hope he would. She wouldn't be going anywhere and if he wanted her, he knew where to find her.

12

Max pushed the button on the steering wheel to end the call with his mother. He ripped out the earpiece and tossed it into the cup holder. His heart hung heavy in his chest. Kara had alluded to the fact that his mother had played a significant role and ultimately changed the course of their lives.

He was stunned. Angry. He didn't want to believe what she'd told him about his mother and he didn't want to believe that his mother could do such a thing and to learn that she had was worse than Kara's not telling him. She should've said something! He would have dealt with it. But no. His mother fabricated a lie and Kara had believed it.

He had some thinking to do.

The women in his life had let him down. His mother for hiding such a bitter secret all these years and Kara for not trusting him enough to tell him. And Caroline, who'd been a rebound and they both agreed it was a mistake, divorcing within months. Not a great track record for building trust and relationships and it explained why he avoided emotional entanglements.

He shook his head, confused and lost in his thoughts. He stepped on the gas, and his truck jumped into higher gear. But with Kara it was different. He'd never stopped loving her, even when he'd been able to shove memories of her to the back of his mind. But he was hung up on her not trusting him.

Anger sat in the pit of his stomach and he didn't like it at all. Distraction--that was what he needed right now and he knew just where to get it. He pointed the truck toward Niagara Falls. A night at the blackjack table would do the trick. It wasn't often he headed there, but before he started his heavy thinking, he needed the thrill of the bet and the sound of the slots to clutter his mind.

What a goat fuck. Everything had gone into the shitter in such a short space of time. But for tonight he'd fill the aching void with a few hours of cards.

It wasn't Vegas by a long shot, but the casinos here would do. A short while later, he handed his keys to the valet. Once inside the casino hall, he cruised past the slots and checked out the waiting list for Texas Hold'em. Too long as usual, so he turned and looked for an empty seat at the tables. Again, all full and minimum bets were now twenty-five dollars. He spied an empty seat and slid onto the stool. The waitress was there in a flash and he ordered himself a draft, double shot of Jack and dropped three hundred dollars on the table. He was never without cash in his wallet, a lesson learned from his father. He piled the chips in front of him and placed his first bet.

Go big or go home. He bet a hundred. His heart jumped in his chest when two aces lay face up, so he split them and hoped for twenty-one. The first card was a nine, the second a face and the dealer busted at fifteen. The crowd around him shouted out and just like that, he was up money.

He tipped the waitress with a ten-dollar chip and settled in for a good night. A few hours and numerous beers and shots later, a commotion at the next table caught his attention. A domestic situation was developing. The guy was hammered, leaning over his cards trying to support his head and making foolish bets while his lady furiously whispered in his ear. But it wasn't all that much of a whisper since the surrounding tables could hear. She expressed her displeasure and told him she was leaving unless he smartened up. He waved his hand at her and she marched away, only to stop and stare at him from ten feet away with her hand on her hip.

Max chuckled, enjoying the scene playing out before him. When she stomped back and gave her guy a shove on the shoulder Max knew there would be trouble. Security wove their way through the crowd and approached the couple from behind. The pit boss must have called them. The guy was going to get tossed on his ass. But rather than abandon her man, the lady stuck up for him and promised to take him from the casino. After much persuasion, he finally slid off the stool and shuffled behind her. She gripped his arm and hauled him across the casino floor, with security close on their heels to make sure they left.

Max sat back in his chair and watched the couple leave with their escort. He missed placing a bet and when his attention was called back to the table, he realized he didn't want to be here anymore. An overwhelming loneliness consumed him. With a sigh, he pushed his chips in to cash out. He'd doubled his investment.

Even though the couple had fought and she was mad as a wet cat, she stuck by her man. The exchange between the couple made Max realize how much he wanted a partner, a significant other...a wife. How everything he'd built around him--the business, his house, the land--was just stuff without someone to share it.. The heavy thinking he thought he'd have to do wasn't necessary after all. He had clarity and all it took was watching the couple at the other table.

He needed to get home, fast. The urgency he felt to bang on Kara's door and take her in his arms burned like a fire in his belly. He stood and wobbled, grabbing hold of the chair.

Whoa.

Too many drinks. Shit! No way could he drive like this. He might be able to manage if he took the back roads slowly, but when he stumbled against a pillar, he knew better than to risk it.

Max was pissed at himself for not keeping track of how much he drank. Kara would have to wait until morning. He needed a room to crash and walked very carefully to the hotel lobby to get one. Lucky for him there was availability. He rode up the elevator, fell through the door and tripped onto the bed fully clothed.

13

———

The alarm jolted Kara out of a sound sleep and she immediately felt sick. She hit the snooze button. *Why did I finish that bottle all by myself and then open the other one?* She rolled over and buried her face in the pillow with a very unfeminine groan. If only she'd just corked it. But she hadn't and now she was paying for drowning her sorrow in the wine Max had brought.

The alarm blared again five minutes later, jarring her and sending her heart galloping. Kara rolled to the side of the bed and eased to a sitting position. She needed water. And aspirin.

She shuffled down the hall to the bathroom in the dark and turned on the tap, letting the water run cold, then gulped down three big glasses. The clink of the cup against the sink was like a gunshot in the early dawn. Not even the birds were up yet. She loved having the bakery, but these early mornings were a killer. Kara rested her hands on the counter and wondered why she was so tender between her thighs. Recollection warmed her blood. Ahh. Max. They'd been amazing together, so much better than all those years ago.

Then everything came roaring back and icy fingers gripped her heart. She reached over to check her phone for messages or texts. Nothing. She'd waited all evening, hoping he'd call, and when she couldn't stand it any longer, Kara broke down and dialed his number. It went to voice mail. Why didn't he answer?

He must be furious with her not to answer a call. Was he ignoring her or was there another explanation? A multitude of thoughts raced around her mind, but she couldn't come up with anything that made her feel even the tiniest bit better.

The bottle of wine from his vineyard had beckoned and she'd poured a glass, which led to two and then to opening the second bottle. She thought she'd feel a little closer to him by drinking his wine. A dumb thing to do, but it sounded good at the time.

Kara had worked herself into a state of anger. She felt used and abused by him. How could he just leave like he did and not call? Or answer his phone? They'd made love and his desertion tarnished their exquisite tryst. She had no knight on a white horse to ride in and kick some ass. No, she'd have to do that herself.

"Oh, God. I'm gonna be sick," she told the dark room and took a breath, holding it. The feeling passed and she let her anger at Max replace the nausea. She had to get dressed and down to the kitchen. On the way back to her bedroom, a sound from downstairs stopped her. A key jangled in the door.

Max! He'd come back. Kara took the old wooden stairs, carefully gripping the banister for support. She was wobbly and most likely still drunk. A light flicked on below. She fully expected to see Max in her kitchen and her stomach dropped when she saw Jilly and Shane setting three Tim Horton coffees on the counter. It wasn't him and it dawned on her he didn't have a key anyway.

"Morning!" Why did Jilly always shout her greetings? Kara's hangover-sensitive ears rang and she cringed.

"Um, morning." She was horrified to be in such a sad state in front of her employees and inched back to the stairs. She noticed them exchange looks and smile at each other. She was thankful they didn't say a word.

"Listen, I'm not feeling so great. Do you mind getting a start on things and I'll be down in an hour or so?"

"No problem, Kara." Shane assured her they'd be fine and she could stay in bed as long as she needed.

"Mm, thanks."

"Here, take your coffee." Shane handed it to her. Kara nodded her thanks and trudged up the steps. Back in her room, she had a big gulp of coffee, took a couple of aspirins and crawled back between the sheets. After a long sigh, she was fast asleep in seconds.

Hours later she woke to birds singing and sun creeping in to shine across her face. She wasn't as quick on the uptake as she should have been, but a whole lot better than earlier. She took a brisk shower, wound her wet curls into a loose bun and had herself together in fifteen minutes. She picked up the cold coffee and carried it downstairs. She was pleased by the sight that greeted her. She inspected the trays lined up and said a silent *thank you* for these two wonderful students who'd dropped into her lap. Shane and Jilly had everything organized and ready to go.

"Hiya, feel better?" Shane smiled at her.

"Yes, much. Thank you. You guys are great and I totally appreciate your help." Kara leaned against the counter, waiting for her coffee to heat up in the microwave. "Thanks for taking care of things this morning."

"Yep. It's all under control." Shane smiled and carried a tray to the front. Kara followed him. It was going on seven and everything would be ready for opening at eight-thirty. Kara helped herself to a croissant and bit into the flaky pastry. The buttery almond flavor reminded her of the words Max had whispered in her ear last night while making love. She shivered, the memory still very ripe and tangible. Her belly fluttered and heat rushed Kara's cheeks. She closed her eyes and embraced her body's response to the memory of them on the lounge. It might be all she had left of him. Her anger had drifted away in her sleep and in its place, bitter disappointment about the turn of events. And acceptance.

What they had done together and how they'd pleasured each other, sharing themselves, touched deep in her soul and she knew it would be imprinted on her forever. Despair filled her mouth with bitterness and soured the croissant. She gulped a mouthful of the Timmy's coffee to force down the lump of pastry.

Now she questioned whether letting him back into her heart and bed had been wise. So many years had gone by and they were different people with very different lives. But maybe those lives could be interwoven? They would have to discover each other all over again all these years later. It could be thrilling and exciting. But that was only if Max was willing.

She finished her coffee and tossed the cup in the recycle bin. Right now, she couldn't let him distract her from her plan. They had a big day ahead of them and she needed to focus. Kara forced out the thought of Max and refocused on the shop. It was the Saturday of the Civic Holiday weekend, and she predicted they'd be swamped.

By noon she was proven correct. They had been so busy there had been no time to think of Max at all or even take a break. Once the lunch crowd dwindled and people stopped to rest their aching feet on the patio, Kara realized there had been no call from Max. She slipped her hand inside the pocket of her apron and touched the phone.

She was dying to call him. Should she? Or give him some space, which he obviously seemed to need. She made a deal with herself to call him at the end of the day. She'd reach out to him then, come what may. She left the phone in her pocket and grabbed a few minutes of peace to do some prep for the wine and cheese appreciation tonight.

A couple of minutes later her phone vibrated in her pocket. Max! She grabbed a cloth, wiped off her hands and ran into the back room to answer in privacy. "Hello?"

"Is this Kara?" The familiar voice turned Kara's belly into a block of ice. "It is."

"Why did you come back and ruin everything?"

"Excuse me?"

"You were supposed to stay away."

Anger flared in Kara. She knew exactly who this was and this time she wouldn't be so easily scared off. "Joyce, I have no interest in speaking with you. Do not call me again."

"You wait, Kara! I want to speak with you."

Kara hesitated and thought quickly. Should she listen to what she had to say? Why not? Information is power and if she was lucky, Joyce might expose herself and her intentions. "What's your problem, Joyce?"

Kara could almost hear her sputter at the other end before launching into a tirade. "You weren't supposed to come back! That was the deal—"

"There was no deal, Joyce. I was young and stupid and you took advantage of me."

"You weren't good enough for my boy back then and you still aren't now." The venom in Joyce's voice hissed through the phone and Kara could almost feel it strike her through the phone lines.

She'd had enough and realized it wasn't worth the effort. Joyce was a bitter old woman who would never be happy and she no longer had any impact on her life. What was done was done.

"Joyce, be quiet. Stay away from me and don't call again. I have no wish to discuss anything with you at all. Goodbye."

Kara disconnected the call in the middle of Joyce's rant. The woman would never change. She refused to let the call rattle her and, in fact, almost felt a sense of relief. That bitch had a way of making Kara feel like an insecure teenager, but not this time and not anymore. She pursed her lips and stuck her chin out. She'd be damned if she'd let her play any role in her life again.

It was curious Joyce would call her today, though. The only logical explanation was that Max must have talked to her. A nervous flutter in her heart made Kara catch her breath. She couldn't even predict what he might do now. It all depended on what Joyce told him. Now more than ever she needed to talk to Max. She dialed his number and it went straight to voice mail.

"Damn. Where the hell are you?"

Frustration ate at her since she couldn't reach him, but

she heard voices in the other room. More patrons. She couldn't worry about it now. There was too much to do before tonight's affair and she needed to be on her game. Kara puffed out a ragged sigh and dropped the phone back in her pocket, blanking any thoughts of Joyce and Max out of her mind.

14

———

1⁴

Goddammit!

He'd arrived home and moments after parking the car heard a huge crash at the end of his driveway.

Max looked at the downed hydro pole that had dragged all the phone and hydro lines with it. Three smashed-up cars littered the end of his laneway, and traffic was backed up to the next concession. His cell phone needed charging but it was impossible with no power, the landlines were out and he was trapped on the property.

Frustration welled up within him. How the hell could he get in touch with Kara except by friggin' carrier pigeon? And he didn't have one of those!

He stood with his arms crossed and watched the lack of activity in getting the vehicles out of the way. Flatbed tows sat waiting for the Ontario Provincial Police to finish their investigation and give the all-clear to move the wrecks. At least no one had been seriously hurt, which was surprising considering the extensive damage.

At the rate they were going, it would be tomorrow before he could get off the vineyard or hope for power. Max tried to calm himself. There was nothing he could do to speed up the process and he hoped word somehow reached Kara about the accident. Then she might understand why he hadn't been able to get in touch with her all day. Now he wished he'd called her before he left the hotel. But he'd been bent on getting to her shop to speak with her in person. The way he took off on her last night, she deserved an in-person apology.

Shit.

15

———

Anticipation twitched along Kara's nerves and she couldn't wait until seven o'clock. The majority of the invites she'd sent had been returned with acceptances, so she was expecting about thirty people, possibly more if those who didn't reply decided to show up. Max had been invited, too, and he had RSVP'd yes. Kara wondered if he'd come and hoped he would.

Shane and Jilly were ready, along with a few student friends they'd brought along to help out. They would handle the food and wine so Kara could mingle with the guests. It had been a long, painful day, but her excitement overtook her exhaustion and she was raring to go. Tonight was going to be fun, entertaining and hopefully very productive.

The jazz band set up their gear on the patio and a carefully worded sign at the entrance stated that it was a private party. Jazzy tunes seeped into the bakery, which they'd transformed into an upbeat wine gastro pub. The newest rage, combining good eats, drinks and tunes.

Kara schmoozed with grace among the guests, ensuring

their every need was attended to. An easy ambience wrapped around her and her guests. Titillating aromas tempted the palate and everything was washed down with a variety of fine Niagara wines. Seductive and cozy lighting totally transformed the bakery into a hot night spot. Kara was thrilled and decided she would make this a recurring event. What a great way to establish We Bake in Heels as the go-to catering company as well as supplier to the area cafés and restaurants. She moved among her guests, satisfied that she'd taken another step on her list of goals.

As the minutes ticked into hours she grew more disappointed Max hadn't shown or called. She steered clear of the wine tonight and whenever she saw a bottle with his vineyard label, Rockpile, her heart hammered and her upset grew. But she couldn't let her emotions intervene with the business at hand and did her best to push Max out of her mind. Once she did, she relaxed again and continued to enjoy the evening.

She carried a tray of goodies to a cluster of people laughing on the patio. "Thanks so much for coming."

"Kara, it's a delight you came home. Why did it take you so long?"

Kara laughed. "Well, it's hard to explain. But I'm so glad I'm home now." And she drifted off to be a charming and savvy hostess to the next group of guests.

Before she knew it, Kara was saying goodbye to her last guest and the night was over .It had proved to be a huge success and she had a list of interested business partners. She waited on the patio while the band packed up and loaded their instruments into the truck at the curb. She waved goodbye and let the quiet night wrap around her.

He hadn't come. She looked wistfully down the street, looking for any headlights that might indicate he was a latecomer. But nothing. She flicked off the patio twinkle lights and closed the doors.

Inside, Jilly, Shane and their helpers finished the last of the cleanup and had even prepped items for the morning bake. Kara took envelopes from a draw and held them out.

"You guys were great. Thanks for all your help." Kara gave Shane and Jilly a big hug and walked them to their car out back. Shane tried to hide a yawn, but Kara saw it and chuckled. They looked exhausted.

"Thank you for this." Shane held up the envelope as did Jilly.

"Don't come in before ten o'clock tomorrow. Sleep in and get here when you can." She felt sorry for making them work such a long day, but they were young and had a helluva lot more staying power than she did.

They climbed into Shane's car and shouted goodbyes, waved and drove off into the night, leaving Kara standing alone in the driveway. She sighed and enjoyed the comfortable sense of well-being that spread within her. It had been a great night.

She leaned back and looked up at the sky. Stars twinkled through the leaves. Max was under the same night sky. Was he thinking of her? Kara shook her head. She was way too tired to do any more thinking herself and couldn't wait to crawl into bed.

Back inside, she let the door swing shut behind her and made a last round before switching off the lights. She paused at the back door to bolt it shut and jumped. A shadowy figure on the other side of the glass startled her at first, but she immediately knew who it was and held her breath.

Kara wanted to rage at him for ignoring her since last night and didn't wait for him to knock. She pulled the door

wide and stood with her hands on her hips, ready to do bat-
tle. He didn't say anything and she tapped her stiletto-clad
foot, waiting to see what he'd say.

"You're mad," he stated simply. "Really? Any reason you
can think of?" Kara was trying hard to be angry with him
and to make him suffer a little bit, but when she noticed
how haggard and worn he looked, whatever tendrils of
anger she held dissolved in the night breeze.

"What's wrong?" Concern edged her voice and she
pulled him inside. He sighed and ran his hand through his
hair. "There was an accident."

"Where? Are you okay?" She looked him over for any
sign of injury and ran her hands along his muscular arms,
relieved that she couldn't see anything.

"Yes, I'm fine. Out in front of my place."

"Was anyone hurt?"

"Thankfully there was nothing serious, but I couldn't
believe the damage."

"Come and sit down." She led him through the kitchen
to the comfy leather chairs out front. At the bar, she poured
them both a glass of wine, which he accepted with a tired
smile.

"I don't think I've ever seen such wreckage before. It's a
miracle no one was killed."

"Tell me." She encouraged him to talk.

He shook his head and gulped the wine. "It was incredible that people walked away with only minor injuries. But
it took forever to remove the vehicles and the congestion.
Power company had to come and fix a broken pole, and so
did the phone company." Their eyes met. "I'm surprised you
didn't hear about it."

Kara shook her head. "No, not a word." She was relieved.

Now she knew why he hadn't called her all day or picked up his phone.

"I'm starved. You've got something to eat in this place, don't you?" He smiled at her and stuck out his long legs, resting one booted foot over the other on the scarred coffee table.

"I think I might be able to find something. I'll be right back." She squeezed his shoulder and was pleased when he leaned back in the leather chair. His chest rose and fell with a big sigh and he looked as if all the tension in his body eased.

She fixed him a big sandwich, selected a few appetizers left over from earlier and set them on a platter. He could pick and choose what he liked. Kara smiled to herself. It was so good to see him resting in her chair, in her shop, looking so comfortable. He had come to her, after all, and reached out for her company despite being so upset. Kara's heart swelled with love for him. The urgent need to take care of and tend to him overwhelmed her.

She didn't bother to turn the lights on, satisfied with the glow the exterior street lights cast into the room, creating a cozy, intimate feeling. He looked very inviting stretched out on the chair and she let the memories of last night rush back.

"Here you go." His eyes were closed when she put the platter on the table in front of him. "Are you sleepy?"

"Thanks." Max sat up with a groan. "This is quite a spread. Yep, I'm kinda tired."

He grabbed her wrist and pulled her down to him, kissing her gently, and then let her go to reach for the sandwich. Kara watched every move he made. The strength in his tanned forearms and hands dwarfed the sandwich he held, reminding her all too well how they'd cradled her last night. Her thoughts quickly ran to the erotic. It had always been hard to stay mad at him, and it was so much better being turned on by him.

They still had to talk; she wanted to know why he'd left so abruptly last night. But, looked exhausted and she decided to broach it later, for now was content to watch him eat. They sat in comfortable silence, noshing on the food until he sat back and patted his stomach. "Thanks, that was great."

"You're welcome." It delighted her when people took pleasure in her cooking. Kara ignored the glass of wine she'd poured for herself and was about to get up for some sparkling water when his hand reached out for her. She halted mid-step.

"Kara, I know what happened," he said in a low voice.

"Pardon?" *What happened when?*

"Mother. I spoke with her last night." She could hear the hurt behind his words, and her heart broke for him.

She drew in a cautious breath. "S-she told you?" Kara hesitated. "Now, after all this time?"

He nodded. "Yes. I know she told you to leave, that you weren't good enough for me." He shook his head with a bewildered look on his face. "And even tried to pay you to leave." He watched her intently.

Her heart stilled, waiting to hear what else he might say. When he didn't, she added, "I didn't take any money from her."

"I wasn't saying you did. Just what she told me," he added quickly.

Kara nodded, unable to form words, and tears pricked her eyes.

"Kara." His voice was so low she barely heard him. "It

kills me that you ran off without talking to me. We could have figured it out."

"I couldn't!" The words burst from her and tears stained her cheeks.

"Why?"

"Oh, Max, come on. We were kids. And you know what she was like. I couldn't believe what she was saying to me." Kara hesitated, trying to contain her feelings. "And she's your mother. What could I do? I couldn't put myself between you." Kara took a long breath. "You knew I wanted to go to Europe, to school. I thought it was the right thing to do at the time."

Looking back now, she should have stayed and told him. But she didn't and it had set both of them on completely different paths. "Then by the time I considered returning, you were married to Patricia. I couldn't come back then."

"Patricia! She told you that?" He shook his head and took a long drink of wine, then met her gaze. "I married Caroline first, after she tricked me, saying she was pregnant when she wasn't." He sighed and waved his hand. "Patricia was a mistake and we both knew it, rectifying it as quickly as we could." He paused and Kara held her breath with all this being revealed. "Well, after the conversation I had with my mother last night, I highly doubt she'll be trying any other manipulations."

Kara was blown away by that revelation. Caroline! Who the heck was Caroline? No, she decided she didn't want to know. None of this was making sense, and honestly, she wanted to leave it all in the past now. Geez, his mother was a piece of work, but in light of all this, she had to tell him, so in a low voice she said, "Your mother phoned today."

"Are you kidding me?" He sat up, his face thunderous. "She just doesn't get it."

"Get what?"

He didn't answer right away, but the intensity on his features caused her breath to hitch. What was he going to say?

"I love you, Kara."

Silence echoed through the room. Had she heard him right? A smile broke wide and she threw herself on him, raining kisses over his face. He loved her!

Kara laughed when his arms reached around and held her tight. His lips found hers and the passion in his kiss spoke louder than any words ever could. She wanted to tell him so much, but she was overcome with joy, with passion, and could only laugh and kiss him back.

Kara shifted so she straddled his lap and cupped his cheeks in her hands, keeping their lips fused together. She recognized the expression on his face when it shifted with his arousal. Their eyes held and it set her heart galloping. He had that special look she'd seen so many times when they were teenagers. She gripped him tighter and her lids fluttered closed.

He loves me!

Kara was giddy with happiness, and the tenderness in her kiss quickly became more passionate. He responded to her demands and his reaction stole her breath. Max's firm grip against the small of her back pressed her intimately next to his belly. The willowy sundress she wore rode up her thighs, leaving only the barrier of her cotton panties and his shirt between them.

"Aren't you tire?" she whispered against his mouth.

"Never too tired for you."

She sucked in a breath at their closeness, but they weren't close enough. She needed more. Kara struggled with the bottom of his T-shirt until she was able to pull it up, desperately needing to feel the heat of his flesh. She thrust her hips forward against the very evident ridge of his erection still trapped within his shorts. She was a trembling mess, and loving every minute of it.

Max's hands caressed her back, over the light fabric of her dress, and moved into her hair. She tipped her head back, baring the column of her throat to him. He massaged her scalp, giving rise to exquisite sensations that shivered through her whole body right down to her toes. It didn't matter where he touched her, it was all so perfect. She moaned in ecstasy, hoping he wouldn't stop.

As if he could read her mind, Max leaned forward and nibbled along the pulsing vein up to her earlobe, murmuring incoherent words, sending more shivery delight radiating over her flesh. He brushed his fingers across her neck, moving her hair aside, and stroked the curves of her ear. Kara ground her hips down on him, feeling herself dampen in readiness. He knew every one of her erogenous zone, even after all these years.

"Oh, Max," she sighed, unable to control her tremulous muscles.

"You're trembling," he whispered next to her ear.

Kara nodded, sucking in her lower lip. "Mm, hm."

"I like that." The husky tone struck a chord with her, making her weak.

She smiled and a deep laugh burst from her lips. She dropped her head forward, and her curls swung around them like a golden curtain. Max thrust his hips up and his cock bumped deliciously against her damp heat. She enjoyed the feel of him next to her, but it was time to get rid of the clothes. Kara reached between them, pulled the zipper down and freed him. It didn't take him long to pull her panties aside, tearing the delicate stitches until there was nothing left to keep them together.

She clenched her thigh muscles and rocked her hips back and forth, sliding deliciously over his cock. Her body jerked slightly every time the tip of him teased against her clit. It roused her further and at the same time readied him for her. He groaned and gripped her tighter, the length of him growing harder with each thrust she made. This time she was in charge and planned to stay on top. She lifted herself and he held her hips steady.

Kara kissed him and reached between them to grasp his cock in her hand. She positioned him, then slowly lowered herself. He filled her and her groan of pleasure expressed everything she felt as he stretched her wide.

She accepted him. Her muscles relaxed and clasped him in delicious tightness. He flexed inside her and gave a deep, guttural groan. A powerful tremor rippled through his body and she rode him. He held her hips tight, their lips fused together, tongues tangling. They rocked in perfect harmony, born to be together.

Kara gloried in his firm muscles and the tickle of hair beneath her fingers. She forgot she still wore the sundress until Max's hands found their way under it and pushed it up. The movement broke their kiss and Kara raised her arms so he could remove it—her bare breasts perfectly in line with his face.

"What a view."

He leaned forward and pulled an erect nipple between his lips. The sensation of his mouth suckling on her, his hard cock buried deep inside and her clit rubbing against him drove her crazy. Kara clutched him tightly and he thrust into her. She matched his stride. They were synchronized in their giving and taking. Her breath suspended, she sucked in little gasps when the wonderful tightening pulses began in her pussy and her muscles clamped around him. She struggled for breath with each thrust and a low moan began in her throat.

"Come for me, baby," he encouraged her, his voice hoarse with desire. Max tensed and groaned. She knew he was close, as was she. She moved her hips, anxious to bring them both to orgasm, and then it was there. The contractions began in a roll of ecstasy, beginning in her belly and dipping lower to her clit. The pulsing carried her into shrouded darkness and then exploded in a rhythmic, pounding glory.

Her cry of delight echoed in the dimly lit room and he gave one last thrust, which sent Kara onto another wave of spectacular bliss. He shuddered in her arms with his own release and a low groan was muffled in her neck. They drew pleasure from each other. Their movements slowed until they rested in each other's arms, spent and satisfied. Finally, they were able to catch their breath, the silence of the room enveloping them in tranquility.

Kara pressed her lips to his neck, just under his ear, and gloried in the pulsing power as his blood continued to rush under his skin. She breathed in his unique scent. How she loved this man, and he needed to know.

"Max."

He hugged her tight and kissed her shoulder. "Yes." His voice was still gravelly with desire.

She shivered with delight and smiled. A throaty laugh bubbled up and she leaned back losing herself in his passion-filled eyes. "I love you." Kara placed a hand on his cheek.

He grinned and covered her hand with his. "I love you, too."

. . .

I hope you enjoyed Max & Kara's story. Second chance romances can be so sweet once the obstacle in their way is overcome. Have you read BACKDRAFT? After a fling a few years ago, a fatal fire brings Andrea and Taylor back together ...

Start your journey into the world of Backdraft **HERE**

Get your complimentary downloadable copy of **My Reading Journal** when you sign up for my NEWSLETTER.

To help other readers discover books you enjoy, while supporting authors, please leave honest reviews.

ALSO BY SHANA GRAY

Shana Gray writes contemporary romance and women's fiction that just might make you laugh. With more than 35 books behind her, some translated into multiple languages, she's always eyeing the next story line. She lives in a small town in Ontario, Canada, is a mom of two grown sons & daughter-in-law, Mimi to a granddaughter & grandson, and human to her rescued Golden Retriever, Hiro. When she's not writing, she can be found cuddling with her grandbabies, daydreaming about life, usually with a glass of wine or cocktail in hand and making travel plans to far off lands to feed her wanderlust.

Shana's Bookshelf – Available Here

Single Title

Working Girl

Backdraft

Northern Rescue

Passion Cowboy Style

Girls Weekend Away Series

What Happens in Vegas – Free eBook

Meet Me in San Francisco

The Nashville Bet

A Match made in Monaco

Harlequin Blaze

A Cowboy in Paradise

More than a Fling

Foreign Translations also available.

Sign up for Shana's newsletter HERE Join Shana's Shananigators group on Facebook

Shana is represented by: Louise Fury

http://www.thefuryagency.com/

The Fury Agency, 5676 Riverdale Ave., Suite 101, Riverdale, NY 10472,